Y0-AGT-174

JOBS & OTHER PREOCCUPATIONS

WINNER OF THE 2000 WILLA CATHER FICTION PRIZE

The Willa Cather Fiction Prize was established in 1991 by
Helicon Nine Editions, and is awarded annually to a
previously unpublished manuscript chosen by a distinguished
writer through an open nationwide competition.

The judge for 2000 was Rosellen Brown.

JOBS & OTHER PREOCCUPATIONS

STORIES

DANIEL COSHNEAR

Winner of the 2000 Willa Cather Fiction Prize

With an Introduction by
Rosellen Brown

HELICON NINE EDITIONS
KANSAS CITY & LOS ANGELES

Copyright © 2001 by Daniel Coshnear

All rights reserved under International and Pan-American Copyright
Conventions. Published by Helicon Nine Editions, a division of Midwest Center
for the Literary Arts, Inc., P.O. Box 22412, Kansas City, MO 64113.
www.heliconnine.com
Requests to copy any part of this work should be addressed to the publisher.

Acknowledgments appear on page 212.

Cover illustration: Terry Fury
Book design: Tim Barnhart

Helicon Nine Editions is grateful to the National Endowment for the Arts,
a federal agency, the Missouri Arts Council and the Kansas Arts Commission,
state agencies, and to the N.W. Dible Foundation and
the Miller Mellor Foundation for their support.

LIBRARY OF CONGRESS CATALOGING-IN-PUBLICATION DATA

Coshnear, Daniel, 1961-
    Jobs and other preoccupations : stories / Daniel Coshnear. -- 1st ed.
      p. cm.
    "Winner of the 2000 Willa Cather Fiction Prize, selected by Rosellen
Brown."
    ISBN 1-884235-34-4 : (pbk : alk. paper)
    1. United States--Social life and customs--20th century--Fiction. I. Title:
Jobs and other preoccupations. II. Title.

PS3603.O69 J63 2001
813'.6--dc21
                                                                    2001031543

Manufactured in the United States of America
FIRST EDITION

HELICON NINE EDITIONS
KANSAS CITY & LOS ANGELES

For Marie Coshnear

Contents

At the height of being in love, the boundary between ego and object threatens to melt away.
—Freud

Hence, also, the product of his activity is not the object of his activity.
—Marx

INTRODUCTION

Daniel Coshnear's *Jobs & Other Preoccupations* is a rough-edged book, which is not to accuse it of artlessness or imperfection but rather to credit it with a quality of edginess, a fierceness and daring that never lets the demands of the "well-made" story protect it from its characters' pain.

The most difficult job represented here, which we visit more than once, puts us in the harried, frustrated, positively Sisyphean company of the staff of The Open Door, a homeless center that serves a group of miscellaneously insulted, injured, incapacitated and mostly futureless residents. They—both staff and "clients"—drown in an acronymic alphabet soup of forms, diagnoses and prescriptions (IR's, PES, SOAPformats, L(iving) S(kills) A(ssessments) and outcomes (overdose, disappearances, suicides). How anyone, on payroll or flat broke and in need of succor, can stay sane in this cauldron of unfillable needs is a miracle. But of course, not everyone does, and the stories that deal with the repercussions of failure are heartbreaking, rendered by Coshnear with poignancy and candor.

Some of the work we encounter is less populated than the world of the Open Door stories. In the first story in his book, "New Job," Coshnear hollows out a quiet place for simple grief and lets us dwell there a moment in silence. But there are stories here, the "other preoccupations" of the title, that don't concern jobs at all, unless childhood, male conversational jousting, a couple engaged in sex therapy, the drama of lust and longing among neighbors, can be construed as work. There is also a good deal of brilliantly mordant meditation on (and convincing demonstration of) neurosis, as witnessed in the analyst's office and free-floating in the atmosphere, a combination of send-up and cri de couer.

If Don DeLillo could compress his angst into a few pages, his story about our unslakeable hunger and thirst would be called "Toxic Round-up," and it would begin like this: "Too many cooks. Too many chiefs. Too many transmissions shifting out of sync. Too many hands in the air. Too many new releases. Too much desperation. There are good germs and bad germs, but too many surfaces. Too many drugs to choose from. Too many missiles, spears, bullets, words. Not enough targets. Too many choices of coffee makers. Too many shoes in the closet." The anxiety level mounts, crests, diminishes; the story ends not with a bang but a desperate perfectly registered whimper.

In fact, Coshnear understands very well that what he demands from a story is his own daring and unblinkered attentiveness. In "Gauge," a writing teacher—there's another job that skewers dead-on—says, "One way of seeing stories is that they are a succession of problems to be solved. The storyteller creates a problem, then solves it. Or doesn't solve it. Some problems are, of course, more interesting than others. The girl's solutions were too neat for me. I'm a sloppy person. Her solutions were creative, sensible, but too neat." (Then with characteristic generosity, he adds "She's young, though." He may be critical, but he's not unkind.)

Daniel Coshnear's stories put their money where their mouth is. Though they certainly are not neat, I wouldn't call his acutely detailed vision and his compassionate but unconsoling honesty, sloppiness. However unfashionable the word, I'd rather call it soul.

Rosellen Brown
Judge

New Job

THE CALL COMES IN SHORTLY AFTER NOON. A woman out in Rio Nido wants her cat put down. It is my first such assignment and I expect they'll send Scott or Chipper with me, but no, Angie says, "Go on, you can handle it." She says, "It doesn't matter who's with you, when you give the injection you'll feel all alone. You might need the time to talk to yourself on the drive back." Angie's in charge and I think it's because she says things like that.

It is the end of fall and it hasn't rained yet; each sunny day feels like a blessing. I've just begun this second career after ten years on the sales floor at Macy's, women's apparel. My weekly pay has dropped by about fifty percent, but I live alone. My needs are modest. I can afford it. What I feel I can't afford is to continue in work that makes me despise people. I should have quit sales when I realized that my biggest satisfaction came from selling to someone I did not like something she did not want. But, I must add, I was damn good at it.

The woman's directions were clear so I have no trouble finding her house. She lives in a three-hundred-square-foot shingled shack under a stand of redwoods. No one in this area can grow grass and most of the lawns are decorated with a muddy ensemble of logs and car parts, but this woman manages a lush, low-growing forest of ivy and juniper. Her house opens from the side and with my Sonoma County Humane Society bag in hand I follow a brick path to the door where she stands waiting.

"I have some tea," she says, "if you'd like some." Her hair is long brown with streaks of gray, the way I imagine mine will look in a few years without henna treatments. Because of a spot of sunlight reflecting off the glass door, I can't see her eyes, but I can see she is tall, an inch or so above me when I reach the threshold. She wears a cable knit sweater and a denim jacket. She is not the sort of woman I frequently saw shopping in the mall.

"Sure," I say, "a cup of tea would be fine." She welcomes me into her kitchen which is tiny and intricate, similar to mine, but it looks as if she's done the carpentry herself. Above the sink are a dozen hand-made cubbies of different sizes, some with wooden doors, knobs painted the soft absorbing gold of sunlight in the trees. Beneath the sink and along two walls are cabinets draped with colorful slips of fabric, the kind you see in those Guatemalan import shops. My eyes follow a purple and blue cotton swath to the corner of the room where I can see a picnic basket lined with a towel. I lean over the edge of the table and find in the basket my first injectee, an emaciated creature, pink and wrinkled but for a few spots of white-yellow fur. In spite of its accommodations, only a few feet from the base of the wood stove, the cat is curled tight and shivering.

She puts tea on the table in front of me.

"You said it has FeLV?" I ask. Feline Leukemia Virus. I haven't forgotten, just feeling the need to say something. I am immediately cozy in her home. I like that I am here with a sense of purpose. I am glad to be working and not in a mall, not irritating some already irritated woman or man with *May I help you*, but here in a real place prepared to offer real help. When I ask about the FeLV, what I want to do is convey a tone of seriousness and concern. I want to know that I can disguise my elation, which under the circumstances would undoubtedly seem inappropriate.

"Yes," she says. I think her eyes are brown, but given the dimness in the room and the steam from her tea, I can't be sure.

"He didn't suffer so long. He was diagnosed three years ago, shortly after my husband died." she looks down into her cup. "It was a slow decline."

"I'm sorry," I say, but I am unclear what about. In any case, I'm not sorry.

"Today is the anniversary of my husband's death," she says. "Bert was his cat. He loved him." Again I feel confused. Who was he and who was him? The woman stands and turns to the sink. She pours out her tea. She hangs her head. A few strands of her hair float in dishwater. Watching her back, I can tell she is trying to breathe evenly. "We'd better get to this," she says, "while I can still do it."

"Yes," I say. "Sure." I set my bag on the table, search the contents again, though I know I have what I need.

"I want to do it in the garden," she says.

"That's fine," I say.

"Can you give me just a couple of minutes?"

"Of course," I say.

"I mean," she sniffs, "can you wait outside?"

"Oh, of course," I say. "I'm sorry." But I'm not, not yet. I step out the door and follow the bricks around to the back of the house. There I see a pond with a pair of orange koi nosing through dark green leaves. Beside the pond is a decayed tree stump, and in the stump she, I suppose, has planted geraniums, pink and white flowers so late in the season. I hadn't seen any clouds when I arrived, but now one passes before the sun and the air is cool and to my surprise she comes out of the house dressed in a threadbare flannel shirt. She cradles Bert in the curve of her elbow. Bert's eyes are closed, but I notice his face beginning to twitch. I suspect it has been a long time since he's been out of doors. I prepare my hypodermic. What is a long time for a cat? Does Bert have any recollection of the man who loved him and died? Does he ever think, this is my lifetime, and soon it will be over? On this last question, I reason no. I reason that that's why we can take it upon ourselves to put animals, as they say, to sleep. Though our nervous systems may be similar, we know pain they can't know. I squirt a single drop of poison in the air.

"Is it OK if I hold him," the woman says.

"Sure it is. But you might have been better off with the sweater and the jacket. He's liable to dig his claws in."

"This was my husband's shirt," she says. "It was Bert that scratched it so thin." She points with her chin to a tear in the shoulder.

"Can you hold him very still," I say. "I wouldn't want to stick you."

She takes short, slow paces to a flat rock on the edge of the pond. With one finger she brushes the remaining fur from the top of Bert's head to the tip of his nose. His eyes open half way. As I poise to give the injection, she says, "Would it kill me?"

"A dose like this wouldn't kill you, but believe me, it'd make you pretty sick."

"What would it take?" She asks.

"It'd take one of us being very careless," I say. "Look," I say, "I know this is hard," and I am beginning to know it, "but believe me, you're doing the right thing." It is with this second utterance of "believe me" that I first see her eyes. They are cold, clear, flecked with green and brown like the water in the pond. They fix on the smile that curls my lips. How many times have I said, "believe me," on the sales floor? I have nothing to sell here, yet it slips out, and with it, my composure. "Believe me," I say again, "you're going to feel better when this is all over."

"I have some idea of how I'm going to feel," she says. "And I don't believe you." By now feeble Bert is nuzzling at her armpit. With one flat hand she presses him tight against her biceps, his chin against her shoulder. "Let's not waste any more time," she says.

"Fine," I say. "If you're ready." I place a thumb on Bert's neck beside the spot where I want to sink the needle. I expect it to feel tough on the surface, then go in very easily, but what I feel is the opposite. I may have hit a bone. Bert's eyes open wide. He claws wildly until his hind feet find traction on her forearm. I fear he'll spring into the pond, die an ugly death. With my free hand I help her hold him secure. Together we feel the life drain from his tiny body.

"Do you want me to take him?" I ask.

"No," she says, "I'll bury him."

There is nothing more to say. I am eager to go, but I don't want to appear hurried. I glimpse her eyes again. She seems miles away. I pack my equipment into my bag. I step back to the brick path and begin toward my car when she says, "I didn't mean to be rude. You understand."

"It's OK." I say, but it is not. I resent her. This is not how I wanted to feel about my new job.

"Have you done this before?" she asks. Her voice is tender. Her face is open now, and kind.

"This was my first," I say.

"Believe me," she says, "it gets easier."

How We Remember You

11/10 OVERNIGHT
  Residents appeared to sleep well through the night.

                                                          Shannon

Staff Meeting Minutes 11/11 Thursday
Present: Jessica, Shannon, Lee, Tony, Danielle.

  Welcome to Tony who joins us officially today. He formerly worked as a residential case manager at The Lighthouse, an ICF for DD adults. He has never worked with the homeless population, but he says that the policies and procedures here at The Open Door look familiar. Jessica has orientation packet for Tony to read and sign.

  State audit could occur any day in the week of 11/21. It will be on-site. In last year's audit the emphasis was on client records–charts–but a brief inspection of the premises was also included.

  Audit Checklist:

* All overdue LSA's (Living Skills Assessments) must be completed and in Jessica's box by 11/17.

* All incident reports must be filed in the IR folder. IR's must be completed, signed and sent to the appropriate recipients w/in 24 hours of incident—no exceptions.

* Need to update med files in back of charts (consult w PES).

* Review charts and replace entries which do not fit mandated SOAP format—Subjective/Objective/Assessment/Plan. Shannon volunteers to assist Tony w SOAP technique.

* Fire extinguishers must be checked for expiration date and pressure. (Lee's job)

As always, residents need to be prompted to complete their household chores.

We can expect an internal audit any day. This is a crucial time as our operating cert is up for renewal and the state is looking to save $ by cutting $ to programs such as The Open Door. Jessica says they're breathing hard at admin. <u>We must be perfect.</u>

Update on resident issues:

<u>Brian</u> admitted 11/9, Axis I impulse control disorder, Axis II 3.170 mild mental retardation, age 39, hx of tantrum behavior, destruction of property, shoplifting. Brian has been homeless in Santa Rosa for at least six months. He was referred to The Door by county psych services. Lee completed the intake. Lee adds: "He likes to watch the 49ers on TV and read the Bible. He's cool."

<u>Kerry</u> appears to be adjusting well here, though she says she's had some "freaky" experiences in shelters before. Seen at Oakcrest on 11/5 and had her Navane reduced to one tab per day at bedtime. No changes noted so far. Kerry gets along well w her roommate, Suzy, and the two of them hope to share an apartment one day. For Tony's benefit, Lee says: "She looks just like Faye Dunaway did in 'Barfly.'"

<u>Suzy</u> is bipolar and staff agree that she is currently in her manic phase. She is extremely upbeat, helpful w household chores, volunteering for special projects, but at times she exhibits signs of anxiety. "Not anxiety," says Lee, "terror." Shannon ordered a med eval at Oakcrest, but Suzy can't be seen until 11/18. In the meantime, Jessica requests that staff observe her very closely and note any changes in mood or behavior. "She's the tall skinny one w blue hair."

<u>Jackie</u> needs several verbal prompts to begin her chore—mopping the kitchen. She frequently appears distracted. Is her forgetfulness a function of a learning disability or PTSD (Post Traumatic Stress Disorder). Shannon says she thought PTSD was something that only happens to war vets and Jessica explains that it has recently become a common dx among the homeless. No new

referrals were recommended.

Jackie is still waiting for her SSI to be rerouted from her NYC address. She is our only black resident right now.

Carl. No change was observed in his depression. Staff disagree re his treatment plan. Shannon argues that all staff should encourage Carl to join in group activities. She fears that his isolating contributes to his low self-esteem and she insists that staff need to be consistent. Tony agrees about the importance of consistency, though he hasn't met Carl yet. Lee's position: (if I'm getting this right) is that "isolating" is "a bogus word" and that "sometimes Carl wants to be left alone like anybody else."

"Carl looks like a potato," Lee says. "A potato w white hair."

Clyde received his first written warning because he called a staff an "insane bitch" when she reminded him to sweep the front porch. Staff agrees that Clyde's paranoia has been on the rise. No one knows whether Clyde has been taking his antipsychotic. For Tony: Clyde has passed thru The Open Door many times, but hasn't yet lasted the full sixty days. Jessica noted that on his last admission to the shelter he was discharged early because of disrespectful treatment of staff, but that on this tour he seems to be doing much better. Shannon says she prefers "insane bitch" to "fucking Nazi."

Clyde has a brown beard and wears bifocals. "You've probably seen him on the corner of Fourth and Mendocino," says Lee. "No," says Tony, "I never get downtown."

Jessica inquired about other issues and nothing surfaced. Residents who were not discussed this week will be considered in next mtg. Lee offered a brief physical description of each for Tony.

Notes by Danielle

11/11 P.M.

Kerry said she saw her ex down at the Drop-In Center. She thinks he's stalking her. Suzy corroborated. I asked her if she wants to get a restraining order and she said, "The cops don't do a damn thing if you're homeless." She said she'll think about it.

Brian was obsessing about his laundry, to use the washer here or to use the coin-op in town which is familiar. Otherwise he seems to be adjusting well.

Tami brought home some painkillers for her ankle. Darvocets, prn, not to exceed 4 x a day. She will self-monitor.

Rosa cooked an excellent meal tonight, chicken enchiladas. Everyone enjoyed.

After dinner I found Carl lying on his bed. I encouraged him to join the others in a game of Risk, but he declined. I reminded him of his social/recreational goal and he said that maybe tomorrow he'd play.

Thanks Jessica for approving my vacation. I'm in desperate need of sunshine.

Shannon

P.S. add Ajax to the shopping list.

11/11 Overnight

The residents appeared to sleep well through the night, blah, blah, blah. I'm so sick of writing that in the charts. I don't know how the residents slept. Let me tell you how I slept.

I had this dream that my old high school girlfriend was admitted here at The Door. It was too real because I was doing the intake and I asked her all the questions that are on the face sheet: Do you have any income? Nope, she says. How long you been homeless? Forever, she says. What's your dx? I'm still sick about you, she says, then she's all over me. But you know how dreams can go. In the middle of some heavy mouth to mouth she grows a mustache and she looks just like my dad and I'm freaking and then, thank God, I hear Suzy banging pots around in the kitchen and I know it's time for me to get up.

I told Suzy thanks for saving my life and she said, no problem. She said she doesn't sleep much so she doesn't dream much, but she used to have some whoppers. Bad dreams made her hair turn white, she said and I said, what made it turn blue? That was

Kerry's idea, she said. And how come Kerry didn't dye her hair blue? Because she saw the way mine turned out, she said.

Hey, who went shopping last time? We're almost out of TP but we're up to our assholes in Lemon Pledge.

Lee

11/12 Friday

Thanks for sharing, Lee, but let's try to keep it clean.

Tony has agreed to pick up some of Shannon's shifts while she is gone. Thanks, Tony. Maybe you can review the orientation packet tonight before you start your sleep-over. All the emergency numbers are posted on the wall behind my desk. Don't be afraid to call me if you have any questions.

Oh, Lee, can you cover the Wed P.M. shift? They're having an inservice on MediCal billing over at admin and the rest of the staff have told me they want to go.

Jessica

11/12 P.M.

Jonathan made dinner, something called Meatloaf Surprise. What's the surprise? A dozen hotdogs submerged in the ground chuck.

Suzy's in a manic phase, all right! Laughing, singing, dancing, she never sits still. This morning she spent almost her entire GA check on a set of curtains for the apt she doesn't have yet. Theo was discharged today. Scheduled an intake interview w Fred Richardson.

Rosa was approved for the H.U.D. rebate. Smokin' Rosa!

Had to give Clyde a second warning tonight. What happened? I couldn't find the med records anywhere and so I called for a room search. Records were found folded in a newspaper on top of the TV, but in the search I found two dozen pizza boxes—you know, the kind that Clyde uses to make his signs out of—in Clyde's closet. A couple of those boxes weren't empty. Ants all over the place. I told Clyde he had to get rid of them and he said he was going to assassinate me.

Danielle

11/12 Overnight

Residents appeared to sleep well through the night. Suzy got up once at 12:30 A.M. When I encountered her she was staring at her hands in the light of the refrigerator. I prompted her to return to her room and she responded appropriately. No other disruptions noted.

Tony

11/13 Saturday
Danielle,

Clyde's behavior toward you was threatening and threats to staff are totally unacceptable. It warrants an incident report. I think Clyde should be discharged, but I'll wait for a team decision.

Received a call today from the Santa Rosa police re Brian. He'd been caught shoplifting at WalMart and apparently when the security guard grabbed his arm, he resisted. The police called here because Brian had the house # in his pocket. Due to confidentiality, I was not permitted to share Brian's dx w police w/out Brian's permission. They put him on the phone and soon after he was released. (See copy of incident report attached.)

When Fred Richardson showed up for his intake he was intoxicated. I explained the house policy re alcohol and suggested that he call back on Monday to reschedule.

Deep cleaning went very well. Of course Suzy was a whirlwind. She disinfected under the sink and wiped down the shelves in the locked cabinets. Even Clyde contributed by sweeping the front walk. Because neighbors were w/in earshot, I asked Clyde to reduce his bizarre verbalizations. I caught this much: Jesus was the product of an alien insemination, as was Bigfoot, and the FBI has known

23

it all for centuries, but has chosen to keep the rest of us in the dark. I reminded Clyde of his goal: to talk about subjects which might be of interest to others, and he told me unequivocally, that never has been his goal.

Tony, the charts looked fine this morning. Remember to sign w your full name and give your degree, B.A. or B.S. or whatever.

Shannon

INCIDENT REPORT

Date of Incident <u>11/13</u>
Client <u>Iversen, Brian</u>
Third Parties Notified:
    <u>X</u> Authorized representative
    <u>X</u> Santa Rosa Police Dept.
    __ Psychiatric Emergency Services

Description of Incident:
<u>Resident was arrested for shoplifting (box of Mr. Lemonheads)</u>
<u>at WalMart at 10:30 A.M. Staff received phone call from Officer</u>
<u>Heinz of the SRPD. With resident's permission, staff explained</u>
<u>to officer the nature of the resident's disability and resident was</u>
<u>released.</u>

Outcome:
<u>Resident arrived home at 11:25 and staff spoke w resident re</u>
<u>incident. Staff and resident worked out a behavior contract</u>
<u>pertaining to stealing and consequences, (see resident's Chart).</u>

    <u>X</u> Report sent to Clinical Director
    <u>X</u> Report sent to Community Care Licensing

Shannon Fitsimmons   11/13
Staff name   Date

1130 Santa Rosa Avenue • P.O. Box 2137• Santa Rosa, CA 95402

11/13 P.M.

Hey Tony, write what you must in the charts, but this here is our book and I'd prefer if we talked like human beings in it. Avoid the following: "prompt," "reinforcement," "appropriate and inappropriate behavior," you get my drift. Never ever say "isolating" unless you're talking about particles. Great to have you on board, man.

And don't get me started on the subject of behavior contracts, Shannon. Like our little Forty-Niner didn't get intimidated enough for one day. Christ.

After dinner, before anyone could sit down in front of the tube, I popped in a George Thorogood and The Destroyers cassette— "Bad to the Bone," "Move It On Over"—and tonight the house rocked. Rosa came out with some Tex-Mex blues and then Suzy and Kerry unveiled the most amazing collection of Motown I've ever seen. Tami was up and bopping on her broken ankle. Even Clyde had something to say about "the harmonic convergence of good and evil," but of course nobody knew what the hell he was talking about.

In the middle of our jam, Suzy started crying. I mean she was all gogo boots and broken-tooth grin having the time of her crazy life, but when Brooke Benton hit the lower registers tears rained down her face.

I asked her what's up and she said nothing and I said OK, but if you want to talk about it we can break up this party in a snap. Later she came into the office where Carl was whooping my ass in Scrabble and she said she hadn't been taking her Lithium. How long? About a week. How come? Because it makes her feel flat, she said. I told her I'd have to write what she told me in the records, but as far as I'm concerned she can do whatever she wants with her meds. Be careful, Suzy, I said. She looked at the floor and said OK. She said she just wants to feel alive on her fortieth B'day.

Lee

11/13 Overnight

Completed bed check at 11 P.M. and noticed that Clyde was not on the premises. He arrived at 11:05 and disrupted the house w pounding on the door. I informed Clyde that he had missed curfew. (See Behavior Warning Response sheet in his chart). I told him to return in the A.M. and discuss consequences w the staff on duty—that I am not permitted to bend the regs on his behalf.

Residents appeared to sleep well through the night.

Tony

11/14 Sunday

Goddamn, Tony! I saw Clyde when I was getting on my bicycle. He couldn't have been more than a minute late. Have you ever spent a night out on the street? Have you? Clyde showed up soaking wet this morning at eight and he crashed until noon.

I don't know what his pizza boxes are all about, but I noticed he'd put four new swastikas on the one he was carrying. With a red marker he'd written, "The Earth Shall Inherit The Meek." Are you meek, Clyde, I asked, because I sure never thought of you as meek. "The lion will lie down with the lamb," he said. OK, I said, but which one are you? "I'm tired," he said.

I've been doing some homework and I've discovered The Man. R.D. (Rockin' Doctor) Laing. Forget cognitive theory. Forget object-relations. This guy was talking about helping people. I can say it in a word: AVAILABILITY. Physical, emotional and psychological availability. When the field was dominated by lab coats who believed that talking to schizophrenics only reinforced their psychoses, Laing was bringing patients off the ward to live in his house. I'll pass his book around at our next rap session.

Lee

11/14 P.M.

Everybody was in a great mood this evening. Thanks Lee. We watched The X-Files—the episode about the Loch Ness Monster–and you should have seen Clyde. He looked like he was in church.

Kerry arrived home after dinner and I noticed she had alcohol on her breath. She'd been doing so well, but of course I had to tell her to leave for 24 hours. She denied she'd been drinking. She slammed the door. I don't think she was real upset, just a kind of a show, but I hate kicking people out.

Danielle

11/14 Overnight

I want to sleep in my own bed. When am I ever going to get laid?

It's morning. There's a strange light coming in the kitchen through the window over the sink. Sun that got trapped in a cloud and carried here from far away. Where am I? Brian stands at the table organizing the contents of his Steve Young lunch box: bag of Doritos, yellow apple, bottle of Melaril, bottle of Cogentin. Clyde appears. A moment's pause. Like me, I think, he's arrested by the smells of breakfast, the sight of soft-boiled egg, the sound of fork on plate. He can't leave the doorway. Enter Carl in a pair of longjohns. He pours Cheerios from our industrial-sized box. He senses it too, tries to ignore, keeps his eyes in his bowl. Kerry waits for the dripping Mr. Coffee, softly tapping formica with a pink fingernail. Where'd she get those fuzzy slippers? Hand-me-downs from the closet at the Drop-In Center? And that pink bathrobe with the frill around the collar? What time is it? What year is it? What am I doing here? Suzy arrives, blue hair tucked under knit hat, brown eyes, chipped tooth, polyester shirt with stallions on it—names it, our déjà vu. "One big happy family," she says. She laughs. We're all relieved. We can laugh about this.

Lee

Hey Danielle, I've got two tx for Albert King on Wed night. I'm working. Want 'em? Take 'em. Call me.

11/15 Monday

Tony you're doing an excellent job. Don't let Lee get under your skin. He's always blasting somebody for something, but the upside is you can talk to him because he does listen. You were right. We don't bend on curfew. We also don't let folks in if we think they've been drinking. We don't tolerate threats or disrespect. When residents fail to complete their chores we give them a written warning. Three written warnings and they're out the door; though we tend to be more flexible on this, dependent upon case considerations. We'll discuss at Thursday's mtg.

Lee, for godsakes I hope you get laid soon.

The rumor at admin is that Alyssa or Dr. Goldstein will be dropping by on Tues or Wed. Be polite, of course. Make sure the house is neat and clean. Help them find the charts they want to see. Try to have Carl engaged in some kind of activity because it doesn't look good if he's sleeping in the early afternoon.

Jessica

11/15 P.M.

Jackie told me some amazing stuff this evening. As you all know she moved from NYC so she could visit her son in jail. She didn't get her SSI. She couldn't pay rent, blah, blah, you know that. She got evicted. What you probably don't know is that the first night she was out on the street she got raped in the dumpster behind Carpet World. It wasn't anybody she knew, just some crazy fuck. Did she call the police? No. Did she see a doctor? No. Now she's worried that she might be pregnant. I sent her immediately up to Memorial, but haven't heard back yet.

Otherwise, this has been a dull shift. Has anyone seen any sunshine? Suzy seemed sad. Maybe she's angry at me for giving Kerry the boot last night. I don't know. She sat on the sofa and watched Funny Cars w Brian. I think she wanted to talk, and I wanted to talk to her, but by the time I finished with checking chores and charting, she was off to her room.

Danielle

Just got a call back from Jackie. Tested neg. Thank God for that.

11/15 Overnight

A few minutes after midnight I was awakened by the whistle of the tea kettle. I found Suzy in the kitchen preparing a cup of hot choc. She claimed she couldn't sleep. I reminded her of house policy re use of communal areas after 11 P.M. and she complied by returning to her bedroom.

Jessica, re your last entry, I would appreciate it if we would discuss standards of professional behavior at our next staff mtg.

Tony

11/16 Tuesday

This morning when I asked Clyde to take the garbage out he snapped me a Heil Hitler salute. I told him I didn't appreciate the gesture and he became verbally abusive—the C word—and that's where I draw the line. Clyde has been discharged. I told him, as he already knows, that he can apply for readmission in one month. He actually set a record for himself. He lasted 52 days this time around. Has he grown less hostile or are we getting soft?

Carl and Jonathan seemed to have made a good friendship. J told me they will try to find an apt. together at Second Step. I phoned Laura and she put their names on the waiting list.

I overheard Kerry saying she plans to go back to her ex. Sometimes women are so damn stupid. Suzy is looking despondent and I suspect it is because she knows she'll need to begin her housing search all over again. She hasn't much money. Of course not taking her Lithium doesn't help matters. We'll wait to see what they say at Oakcrest on 11/18.

Hey, the house looks excellent everyone. Great work. Lee, you owe me two Living Skills Assessments.

Jessica

11/16 P.M.

A calm, quiet evening. Kerry prepared fish-sticks, fries, and three-bean salad. Brian needed some assistance w clean up and at my request Jackie assisted. Carl isolated in his bedroom after dinner. My attempts to get him to join a group activity were unsuccessful. Suzy's affect has not changed: depressed.

I spent most of the evening going through charts in prep for the audits. If the state auditors are like those I experienced at The Lighthouse, we can anticipate trouble.

Tony

11/16 Overnight

Kerry kind of freaked out during the night. She said she was missing twenty bucks from her purse and she wanted me to do a room search, but I said I wasn't going to wake everyone up. She said I ought to at least check Suzy's pocketbook. I said I wouldn't. There'd be no way I could tell it was Kerry's twenty even if I found one. Suzy looked blank. She asked me if she could sleep in the living room. I said OK, just for tonight. She said I wish Lee was here and I said, yea, me too.

In the morning Suzy was gone. I don't know what time she left.

Danielle

11/17 Wednesday

What a dull morning. Is it the clouds? Does the house need paint? What? I had hoped Alyssa and Dr. Goldstein would have dropped by so we could be done w the internal, but alas, not yet. Be prepared, Lee. You can call me at admin if something comes up.

When we get through w the state audit, let's do something special. I'm open to suggestions.

Jessica

11/17 P.M.

So who's on the porch when I get here but our internal audit team. Shit, I think, I'm not even going to have time for a smoke. Hey Alyssa, I say. Hey Leo. I've known the guy for five years and he tells me to call him Dr. Goldstein. Punk. I had my heart set on a raucous birthday party, lemon frosting, Otis Redding, but the two of them kept me tied up in the office for hours. Suzy wasn't exactly in top form this

11/17 Overnight

Suzy overdosed. She died.

Lee was here writing in the log when I came in, when Kerry screamed. He tried to resuscitate Suzy. She was like sitting on the floor w her back against the bed. Her eyes were open and one foot was pulled up under her and one hand was on the night table. She looked like she was trying to help herself up, but her body was stiff. I called an ambulance. I called the beeper. I called Jessica. I called every damn number on the wall. There was nothing to do. Lee slapped her face and shook her shoulders. He pinched her nose shut and tried mouth to mouth. He kept trying like—

One of the EMT's said she probably died around 9 P.M. Lee left w Suzy in the ambulance. No one slept through the night. That's all for now. I'm exhausted. I feel sick.

Danielle

Staff Meeting Minutes, Thursday 11/18
Present: Jessica, Danielle, Tony, Shannon

Under the circumstances it is agreed that we abandon the usual format. Jessica recommends that we talk about what happened. She tried to call Lee many times, but there has been no answer. Coroner's report confirms what EMT's told Danielle last night. Suzy died of pulmonary arrest at approx 9:15 P.M. According to the report she had a BAC of 0.16. Combination of etoh and propoxyphene napsylate (Darvocet) was given as the cause of death.

Suzy left no note, and as far as we know, she gave no warning of her intent to commit suicide.

Re the other residents, Danielle explains that Lee woke them all. He shouted "Suzy, Suzy, Suzy" until everyone was standing around the doorway of Suzy's bedroom. He wouldn't stop, says Danielle. Everyone else had given up and Lee kept shouting.

After the ambulance left, Danielle sat w some of the residents in the living room. Kerry blamed herself for not having been a better friend to Suzy. She was hysterical for hours. Jackie held Kerry's hand. Tami blamed herself for having left her Darvocets on her dresser where anyone might get them. Carl made hot choc. He said a prayer in Hebrew. Brian said that suicide is a sin. Jonathan said that birthdays can be a curse. Kerry said repeatedly that she should have seen this coming. She should have been a better friend.

Tony wonders if there is family who should be notified. According to Suzy's chart, there are none. Tony inquires about the results of the internal. Danielle wants to talk more about what happened. She feels terrible. Couldn't we just talk a little about Suzy?

Tony says that people have to be prepared for crises in this kind of work.

Jessica says that it is perfectly legit to talk about these kinds of things when they happen. That talking about feelings is a part of our work.

"I liked Suzy," Jessica says. "When she was up she really brightened our house."

"I thought she was very cooperative," Tony says.

"I liked the way she danced," says Danielle. "I remember when she dyed her hair. I thought she was doing so well. She and Kerry were going to get a pad of their own. Suzy always told me I was a groovy chick. I can't believe this happened."

No one seems to have anything to add at this juncture.

Re the audit, Dr. Goldstein left a set of corrections in Jessica's box. On the site inspection we fared well, but they are not typically thorough in this area. Client records, specifically Lee's entries, were often not consistent w the mandated SOAP format. Several LSA's were missing from the charts.

Jessica asks for volunteers to help fix charts before the state audit. This ought to be Lee's responsibility, she says. Tony and I volunteer. Danielle asks for time off, unspecified.

Re Suzy's death, an incident report must be written. Lee must do it, says Tony, because he was the staff on duty. Jessica will write the IR if she does not hear from Lee by 3 P.M. Still, Lee will need to sign it, says Tony, according to regs. That's a Level I citation, he says. Needs to be w/in 24 hours, I add.

Jessica says underline: <u>If Lee does not appear before 11 P.M. and sign off on IR, he can count himself out of a job</u>.

Notes by Shannon

INCIDENT REPORT

Date of Incident <u>11/17</u>
Client <u>McCloskey, Suzanne</u>
Third Parties Notified:
   <u>X</u> Authorized Representative
   <u>X</u> Santa Rosa Police Dept.
   <u>X</u> Psychiatric Emergency Services

Description of Incident:
<u>Resident was found dead in her bedroom at 10:55 P.M. It was apparent to me that resident had attempted to terminate her life because on the floor beside the bed was an empty bottle of pain-killers which had belonged to another resident.</u>

_____

_____

Outcome:

I attempted CPR, but the resident was deceased. A second staff
called an ambulance and made other emergency notifications as
required. I accompanied the EMT's to Memorial Hospital.

_____

_____

_____

    X Report sent to Clinical Director
    X Report sent to Community Care Licensing

_____

Staff name   Date

1130 Santa Rosa Avenue • P.O. Box 2137 • Santa Rosa, CA 95402

11/18 P.M.

After dinner and chores were completed, I informed residents
that anyone who wishes might come into the office and speak w
me re last night's incident. No one accepted the offer. I assumed
everyone was exhausted.

Kerry asked when she would be able to talk to Lee and I
explained that Lee's status here at The Open Door is at present
undecided.

Tony

11/18 Overnight

At approx midnight, I heard a knock at the door. It was Lee. I
told him he had come at an inappropriate hour, but he insisted on
entering the office. Attached is his incident report. No other
disruptions noted.

INCIDENT REPORT

Date of Incident_____
Client_____
Third Parties Notified:
   ___Authorized Representative
   ___Santa Rosa Police Dept.
   ___Psychiatric Emergency Services

Description of Incident:
<u>I remember you dancing, Suzy. I remember you fighting with</u>
<u>Kerry over the Jackson Five cassette and before I could get it</u>
<u>out of your hand and into the tape player, you were bumping</u>
<u>and grinding to the song in your head. Your hair was braided</u>
<u>and swinging like a horse's tail. You tucked your elbows in tight</u>
<u>against your ribs as if you could compress all the sound down</u>
into your hips and your knees and stomp it out your boots. You
Outcome:
<u>wanted to feel alive and nothing less and I remember you</u>
<u>standing at the gate, me on the porch with fucking Leo in the</u>
<u>office calling my name and you calling, laughing, holding up</u>
<u>your broken sandal by its strap—you were flying. You wanted to</u>
<u>dance. You were drunken sunshine. "I'm forty but I feel like I'm</u>
<u>fourteen," you said, and I said, "Go lie down," and you said,</u>
"But Lee, Sweetie, it's my birthday and I want to celebrate," and
I said, "You fucked up." I said, "Go sleep it off." I went into the
office and closed the door. Suzy, I fucked up. Suzy, I am sorry.
   ___Report sent to Clinical Director
   ___Report sent to Community Care Licensing

<u>Lee</u>_____
Staff name   Date
<u>1130 Santa Rosa Avenue • P.O. Box 2137 • Santa Rosa, CA 95402</u>

*   *   *

11/22 Monday

Thank you Jessica for allowing me some time off. Good luck everybody. I've been trying to reach Lee, but have had no luck yet. I'll call in at the end of the week. I guess I'm just stuck or something. Like I'm trying to remember why I got into this work in the first place. And maybe it's all the rain, I just don't know.

Danielle

*   *   *

11/26 Friday

Welcome back Danielle. Congratulations everyone. Shannon, Tony, Peter, excellent work. We passed the state audit. Alyssa said she's never seen such a high score. We had only one citation and it was a Level V—one of the fire extinguishers was not fully charged.

Let's do something special. I'm open to suggestions.

Jessica

The Right-Hand Man

Sometimes Jasper's horny, and that's a little strange, like the days when he sleeps late and Tim knocks on his door to get paid and Jasper's got an erection under his shorts. If it were Tim, he'd make more of an effort to hide it. Or like when it's hot and Jasper offers to hose Tim down. He says, "I bet you'd like this, Timmy." And Tim says, "You're nuts." And Jasper laughs his crazy laugh. One time Tim said, "Keep dreaming, old man," and Jasper gave him an earful about what's old and what's young. He said, "I might be fifty, but I can still outpace any of the studs in this town." He was serious.

Tim does odd jobs for Jasper who lives in Forestville on the other side of the river where houses are older and bigger than they are in Tim's part of town. Jasper is gay. He's six-foot-two. He dyes his hair black. He was a bank manager and now he's retired, except that he's the landlord of his property. There are three units in all and Jasper lives in the center, called Unit One. Weeds kind of piss him off, so one of the jobs Tim does for Jasper is pull weeds. Tim built redwood fences around the three garbage areas and around the blue gas tank Jasper calls Big Willy. He painted the exterior of the apartments, peach on the wood shingle and lime green on the trim. He spread five yards of rock around Jasper's front and back. It was orange when he put it down but after the winter rains it turned pink and white except where the lawn touches the fence and around the bases of the big oaks. Every couple of weeks Tim drives Jasper's garbage to the dump in his '79 Mazda pickup. Tim says, "I don't have the skills to be a carpenter or anything, but I'm learning as I go and when it comes to keeping this place looking sharp, I'm Jasper's right hand."

Jasper's OK. Tim likes him. He's funny. He's got this laugh that sounds like bubbles rising in a water cooler. And he's generous. Sometimes he throws his money away, like the time he hired a team of idiots to put in his hot tub at thirty bucks an hour per guy and they didn't level it level. They buried the motor in a wall so that if it breaks Jasper'll never be able to get to it without tearing up his kitchen. They screwed him over big time, but that's his business. He pays Tim ten an hour and he always rounds it up, like if Tim works four and a half hours Jasper pays him for five.

Jasper's easy to talk to. Tim doesn't have to say much. Jasper likes to carry on about his begonias or about his never-ending war with the snails. He likes to talk about the Corvette he owned when he lived down in Santa Monica and worked at the bank. He moved from the fast lane into the slow lane, he says, but he's happier where he is. After he told Tim that, he called him an anomoly.

"What's that?" Tim asked.

"I wish I could be more like you, Timmy," Jasper said. "No ambition."

Tim will be eighteen in a couple of months. He's married and he has a baby girl. Besides working for Jasper, he puts in about fifteen hours a week at Gold's Gym in Santa Rosa as what's called a personal trainer. He tells people: "If you want to harden your abs, do some crunches. You want biceps? Do curls. Do lots of reps and build up your weights gradually or else you'll get hurt. But hell everybody knows that," he says, "so mostly I go to the gym, put on their uniform and do my own workout which makes me feel good, like I'm in control for a change." And that's fine if Mr. Rick, the branch manager, isn't around.

One time Jasper was making some cracks about a hole that Tim had in the backside of his working shorts. The tenant from Unit Two, Mars, who also happens to be Jasper's oldest friend, was standing there with him on the deck. "Whew," Jasper said, laughing. "Why don't you pull up some of these weeds over here, Timmy?" Tim didn't know what was up until he heard Mars laugh and say, "Stop it, Jazz," just the way Tim's mother would have said it. Mars lives by that rule: If you can't say something nice, don't say anything at all.

Mars has AIDS, Tim felt ninety-nine percent sure. He figured it out on his own. When Jasper introduced Tim to Mars, Tim thought Mars just had sensitive skin on his face and head. It was blistery with dry patches on his cheeks that looked like they would flake off with a good hard scrub. But besides that, Mars wasn't skinny or anything, not at first. Tim knew a little about the tenants from their garbage, and once he found a white plastic bag behind Mars' unit with more than a dozen empty medicine vials.

Whenever Mars talked to Tim their conversation went the same. Tim'd be up on the ladder priming the eaves or pounding nails into the sheathing that the heat and moisture had pushed out and Mars would be taking a load of something, usually cat litter, to his garbage. Mars'd kick it off with: "What a glorious day."

"Yea, it's nice," Tim'd say. "Not too hot."

And Mars'd come back with, "We're so lucky to have these beautiful summer days." He'd describe how the fog rolled up the river from the coast and dissipated in the early morning sunshine leaving glistening drops on the leaves of the laurel trees. Or if it was later in the day he'd remark about all the colors in the sunset. Big pillows of clouds lit up pink and gold against a sky that was purple to the east and a perfect baby blue out toward the sea. Mars'd sigh deeply.

Tim got bored with it. He knew Mars was a nice guy and he thought that if he ever smoked some bad shit and found himself having a panic attack, Mars was the kind of guy he would want to talk to, but most of the time he preferred talking to Jasper who had a little bit of an edge and who sometimes cracked Tim up, the things he'd say.

The first time Tim went to the dump he rode shotgun in Jasper's fire-engine-red four-by-four pickup. Before they left Jasper was giving Tim hell about a little scratch on the bumper he thought Tim'd made with a wheelbarrow. Tim simply said, "I didn't," but Jasper carried on about the cost of having the thing painted and how many hours of work it would take Tim to pay it off and then about the idiots with the hot tub and then a story about how he'd gotten screwed on his taxes until, even Tim could see that the scratch had nothing to do with himself, except that he should know that Jasper was nobody's fool.

Once they got going, after Jasper felt satisfied he'd made his point, he told Tim a story about an unusual medical exam he'd had—a cystourethroscopy. He spelled it for Tim. This is how they got onto it: Jasper asked Tim about the birth of his baby girl and what it was like being there. "For a little while the pain changed my wife's face so I almost didn't recognize her," Tim said. "I didn't think she was going to die. I couldn't think that." It was impossible to know if Jasper was paying attention because the load in the trailer was piled high and he frequently had to look out of his side view mirror to see if anything was blowing. Tim added, "I just couldn't imagine pain like that."

Jasper said, "I could. I had no idea what I was getting myself into. A little discomfort when I urinated, a little swelling, I thought I ought to get it checked out. Before I knew it, I was strapped in a chair with my legs open while this big German nurse held me in a full nelson and the doctor shoved a metal rod up the hole in my cock. They used a gel that was supposed to lubricate, but it only made it burn worse. They gave me a local." Jasper took his hands off the steering wheel to show Tim the size of the hypodermic they'd stuck in his penis. "I almost passed out from the pain."

"Shit," said Tim, "I don't know if I even want to hear this."

"When it was all done, the doctor told me I might feel a little discomfort the first time I pee," Jasper said. He repeated the phrase, "a little discomfort" three times, louder each time until Tim began to wonder if Jasper thought he was talking to his doctor, except that Jasper had been laughing so hard.

"My plumbing was all fucked up. I felt an awful pressure and I pulled into a Chevron to take a leak. When it finally came, it came with an explosion, blood on the walls, knocked me flat on my back."

"And the funny part," with Jasper there was almost always a funny part, "was that I was in such a hurry to squirt that I forgot to lock the bathroom door. Some nutty kid with shades and a Walkman pranced right up to the john without ever looking down. He stepped on my goddamn stomach! The kid screamed louder than I did!" Jasper was choking from laughter.

"Sounds like that one horror movie," Tim said, "where there's this high shrieky noise and blood swirling down a drain."

"Well, I know about pain," Jasper said.

"Yea, I guess you do," Tim said.

And Jasper said, "You bet I do!" He took his eyes off the curvy road back from the dump to look hard at Tim's face, like that was going to make it sink in. Tim understood why Jasper wanted to impress him that he was nobody's fool, because he worked for Jasper and all; but this other message, Tim couldn't exactly see the point of.

In the time that Tim worked for Jasper, there were two different occupants of the apartment on the left side of Jasper's, Unit Three. Three has the same number of square feet as Two, and it goes for the same price, but it doesn't get any sun until late afternoon, and that comes filtered through a neighbor's willow. It always smells musty, even after the time Tim scrubbed it with

Pine Sol and left the windows wide open.

First in there was this very stuck-up woman, or maybe she was just shy. She must have been about thirty. She was a little bit fat and she had bleachy blonde hair that she kept wet and combed back. She wore tight jeans and usually a pair of clogs that made her about an inch taller than Tim.

Once, when Tim was painting the wall behind her gate, she didn't have the clogs on and he didn't hear her coming. They were both startled, but instead of laughing and introducing herself, she walked inside and closed her door hard. About an hour later, she passed again and she surprised Tim with a sunny smile, not just lips. Her whole face turned kind. She said she was sorry if she'd scared him.

Tim was glad that she'd apologized because it was getting hot and the paint was hard to spread. The work can go fast when you enjoy what you're thinking about, and it can go the opposite too, real slow when you're pissed off.

Tim had started the day with pulling weeds in Mars' backyard and Mars came out with the usual, "Oh I can't believe this glorious day."

"Yea," Tim said, but he wanted to be back in his bed. He and his wife had been kissing and touching and were just about to get down to it when the baby woke up screaming and they had to stop. Tim left the house mumbling, "I don't ask for much and I never get it anyway." He really couldn't buy into this "glorious day" bullshit.

"Would you look at that lush Magnolia tree," Mars had said. Tim looked up but said nothing. He had a pain in his lower back and he felt like one of his hamstrings was on the verge of cramping. Mr. Rick at Gold's had told him he'd lose his job if he couldn't sign two new members before the end of the month, and Tim's response was to overdo it on the squat machine. Sometimes he liked working for Jasper better than working at the gym because here at least he could let his thoughts run free, most of the time. He grabbed a handful of thorns and hollered, "Shit."

"Those are the worst," Mars said, pointing to the swirl of blackberry brambles. "If we let it go for a couple of weeks it's like the Congo back here." Tim had to laugh. He was reminded of a game that he and his brother played as kids. "Running Through the Congo," they called it. They'd peel branches from the neighbor's forsythia and call them machetes and they'd slice their way through a pair of overgrown hydrangeas to the wire fence at the back of the yard.

"I'm looking out for the dreaded tsetse fly," Tim said.

"Oh, those tsetse's are bad news all right," said Mars, "but don't forget about the leeches."

"Leeches, I can't take," Tim said.

"I think you have to burn them off," Mars said, "or else they leave their leechy little heads in there." And then Jasper came crunching around the gravel on the side of the house, his shorts a little swollen up as usual.

"What are you guys smoking pot back here?" he said.

"Tim's on the trail of the great boa," Mars said.

"I'll show him a snake," Jasper said, and Mars said, "Oh, why don't you stop."

It was then that Jasper told Tim that "that woman"—that's how he referred to the tenant in Unit Three—would be moving out soon. Tim sensed that Jasper didn't like her, but he never knew why. He assumed that as a gay man, Jasper had very little reason to be interested in her, or in women in general. He hadn't thought hard about it, it was just something he'd pondered while pulling weeds.

"You should see the cat food pressed into her kitchen linoleum," Jasper said to Tim and Mars. The face he made when he said it, you'd think his mouth was full of coffee grounds.

In the days that followed, Jasper had Tim scrub and paint the interior of Three. It wasn't nearly so filthy as Jasper had made it out to be, Tim thought, as he was spreading white latex along the baseboards, and he wondered if he might not have liked "that woman" better had it not been for the way Jasper always spoke about her. These considerations led Tim into a familiar and unpleasant train of thoughts, namely: How often do I think for myself? Soon I'll be eighteen. When will I start to feel like a man? Soon, he said to himself, maybe I'll take the test and get my G.E.D.

Next into Unit Three was a family that didn't last long. They were loud and sloppy and they put their dogshit into the garbage unwrapped. The man claimed to be a subcontractor of some kind, but he was often home in the middle of the day. He reminded Tim of Homer Simpson, the way he called everybody, even Jasper, "Babe." The man's wife had big freckles and severe sunburn stripes on her back. She had a pretty good figure, Tim thought, for someone who always had a beer in her hand. Once Tim had taken it upon himself to tell their little boy not to throw gravel at their dog and the woman stared at Tim with dull eyes, and then, as if snapping out of a trance, she grabbed the boy's wrist and smacked the back of his head with her beer can and shoved him through the door into their apartment. Tim wanted to say something to her, but he had no idea what.

One evening after the sun had dropped below the top of the redwood fence, as Tim was refitting a segment of aluminum rain spout onto the edge of the roof, he overheard Jasper tell Mars: "I can't stand the little brat crying all night long any more." Jasper said, "I want that white trash off my property, pronto." And that's what happened. It would have been Tim's job to scrub and repaint the unit, had he not cut the palm of his right hand on the edge of the spout, a two-inch gash that required eighteen stitches.

Tim stopped working for Jasper for two months. In that time he lost his job at Gold's Gym. So what, he thought, he couldn't use the bench press or curl machine anyway. But he would have liked to use their slantboard to do some crunches. As the family's finances went, Tim's injury proved not to be an inconvenience at all. Tim's wife doubled her shifts waitressing at the Brew Pub in Rohnert Park, and she earned almost twice the hourly pay that Tim had earned. What hurt Tim, besides the dull ache in his right hand, was that he was no longer the household breadwinner, not even an equal partner. If his pride were a muscle, he would have put ice on it.

Tim had often said he'd like to have more time to spend with his baby girl, but he was really very happy with the amount of time he'd had with her. When he was working, he'd come home in time for dinner, then it was his job to wear the baby out before bedtime, play wild like daddies are supposed to do. He liked to take her up to Armstrong Redwoods and play hide and seek. She would always hide in the same hollowed out tree trunk, and he never tired of feigning surprise when he found her there. Sometimes he would spy her standing and waiting, her fingers pointed down at her sides, knuckles pressed together, her little chest beating like a bird in a net. God, could she shriek.

But spending day after day alone with a baby was another matter. With only one good hand, trying to pin diapers on her squirming little torso challenged Tim more than some of his hardest workouts. Persuading his little girl not to comb applesauce through her hair, not to push flower pots off the railing of the deck, not to put pennies in her mouth, was more exhausting than shoveling rock or doing one hundred marine style push-ups in the sauna. If such things as patience, imagination, and compassion could be thought of as elements of fitness, then Tim trained harder over those two months than he ever had in his life. On his eighteenth birthday, Tim's wife brought home a bottle of champagne from the pub. After his second glass, Tim started weeping. He didn't know what he was feeling, so he couldn't explain it except to say, "I'm afraid I'm getting soft."

Tim didn't expect to get sympathy from Jasper when he

returned to work. That wasn't Jasper's style. All Jasper said was, "I don't know if I can trust you to go up on a ladder, Timmy. Do you think you can pay attention to what you're doing?" Tim wanted to say, "Kiss my ass," but all he said was, "Sure." Jasper had plenty of work and Tim was glad to be back.

Jasper wanted Tim to shovel up the rock he'd spread and put sheets of plastic underneath it. Weeds had popped up all over. And of course there was the garbage, which Jasper wanted Tim to start with. And then there was a little bit of touching up in Unit Three.

"You mean you haven't rented it out yet?" Tim said.

"No," said Jasper, "and it's costing me a hell of a lot of money."

When Tim began working for Jasper, he thought maybe Mars was Jasper's lover. They were screwing down a plywood subfloor in Mars' unit and Mars said to Tim, "Jazz can do it all." He sounded like a doting wife. And then later when Tim was sitting outside eating a high energy bar, Mars walked onto the porch and said, "You know Jazz's been working on this house for five years. I'm so glad he's finally going to get it finished. What a relief it'll be for him," and he sighed that same sigh that always came after, "What a glorious day."

It seemed to Tim that Mars was kind of living off Jasper, and this he thought even before he knew Mars was dying. Whether they were once lovers or not, Tim couldn't figure, but he doubted it. Sometimes he could overhear them talking on the back deck while he painted. It wasn't so much the words he heard, but the sounds of their voices that helped him understand the true nature of their relationship.

Jasper was always up and down, pacing, laughing, shouting, whispering, even weeping, telling his adventures, which Tim gathered to be mostly about dating. And Mars was like the high school girl with pimples and braces who never got any action but had the good advice. Mars always sat and listened and responded until Jasper was ready to go inside. The two of them would sometimes talk from when the sun was at the top of the sky till the timer turned on the porch lights.

So Tim started with Mars's garbage as he often did, but he was going slow because when he'd make a fist he'd get a pain that shot through his hand and up his forearm. Mars came around to the back of the house with a white plastic bag in his hand and set it on the garbage pile. In the two months that Tim had been gone, Mars'd lost twenty pounds. The rash on his face had spread down his neck, red and raw. Tim tried not to look shocked, but the first thing he thought was, that's a ghost. "Hey Mars," he said.

"Hi Tim," Mars said very softly. He turned around and walked back to his door so quiet on the gravel like the sound of someone eating cereal in the next room. Then he knocked on the window and waved for Tim to come inside.

Mars had always kept his place spic and span, but now it looked like he'd left the housecleaning to the cats. The sink was piled with dishes and the bed piled with clothes. Tim smelled something like old boiled broccoli. "I'm sorry for the mess," Mars said, not in the voice that Tim knew, warm and silky. He sounded like he was under water.

"So what's up, Mars?" Tim said. He wanted to say something that would show he felt sorry, but he didn't know how to say it. Mars took a couple of chrome bars out of a bag. They came with brackets and screws and instructions. He said, "I want you to put these around my bath tub. Some time when you have time."

"Sure," Tim said.

"I'll pay you for it," Mars said.

"OK," Tim said. "But Jasper's the landlord." Then he heard a loud fast crunching that he knew was Jasper.

"Timmy?" Jasper called from out in the yard. Mars walked away into his kitchen.

"Yea," Tim said.

"I've got something important for you to do," Jasper said. "Pronto." Tim followed him around the front past the begonias. Jasper was in a no-bullshit kind of mood. He handed Tim a green plastic bag and a pair of gloves. He pointed along the base of the redwood fence where once there'd been lillies and now nothing but onion grass and clover. "I've got somebody coming to have a look in one hour and I want all the weeds out."

"That's great," Tim said. "So you might finally find somebody to fill this space."

"Use the trowel if you have to. I want them up by the roots."

"What about the garbage?" Tim said.

"Later." Jasper started back toward his own apartment.

"Hey, Mars looks terrible," Tim said. Jasper stopped, but he didn't turn around. If he said anything, Tim couldn't hear it. Then he walked on and Tim heard his door close.

Tim got down on his hands and knees and pulled. With a little practice, he found that his left hand was almost as quick as his right, which he used to hold the bag. Yea, it felt good to be back at work. He smiled when he thought about making love to his wife. He was even feeling pretty damn good about the baby, who'd decided to sleep in for a change. The only thing that didn't sit right was his feeling about Mars. Like Mars shouldn't be alone in his unit right now. Poor Mars who always listened, but had no one to sit and hear about his pain.

Tim heard a crunch on the gravel, not heavy or light, then a British accent from the other side of the redwood fence. "Oh goodness, I must be early." Tim put down his bag and opened the gate. There stood a tall, thin, muscular man in nothing but silk boxers and a pair of Reeboks.

"Hi," said Tim.

"What a lovely garden this will be," the man said, looking over Tim's shoulder. Jasper banged through his door and almost leapt down from his porch.

"You must be Nigel." Jasper was so excited he looked like he was going to pop. As he led Nigel into Unit Three, Tim noticed that the two men were equal in height and had similar builds, though he guessed Nigel was ten years younger. Tim returned to pulling the onion grass. He could hear Jasper telling stories and laughing his crazy laugh. Then he told Nigel to take all the time he wanted and he returned to Unit One.

Soon after, Nigel pulled the apartment door closed behind him and said farewell to Tim. He stopped at the gate and bit delicately on the flesh around his fingernail.

"Is Jasper still here?" he asked.

"He should be in his apartment," Tim said.

"Well maybe you could tell me," Nigel said. "When could I have a look at Unit Two?" Tim didn't know what to say. It seemed he never knew what to say, but this question came as a complete surprise.

"Never mind," said Nigel, "I'll give Jasper a call this evening."

Tim felt as if the remaining weeds were pulling back, and now both of his hands were cramped up. His whole body suddenly ached and he said to himself, "Christ, I'm in awful shape," but that's the way feelings registered with Tim, at least at first. He needed a break, a change. He'd ask Jasper if he should go ahead and do the garbage now, he thought. Or, he'd ask him when he should put the chrome bars around Mars' bathtub. That was what he really wanted to know. Then he could come back to work and get into the flow of it, let his thoughts run free.

Tim knocked on Jasper's door. "I was wondering—" he said, but Jasper either didn't hear or was preoccupied.

"Can I ask you something?" Jasper whispered. He had never spoken to Tim this way before. There was no need to whisper.

"All right," Tim said, but something felt very confused.

"What do you think of Nigel?" Jasper now bent to Tim's height. His eyebrows were high and his eyes were full of anticipation.

This was the Jasper that Tim had so often seen talking to Mars.

"I don't know." Tim said, "He seems like a nice enough guy."

"No, but do you think he's cute?" Jasper asked.

The best Tim could manage was, "Well, I don't know him, do I?"

"You're a lost cause," said Jasper, straightening. "You're hopeless. Go on and get back to your weeds." He laughed his crazy laugh.

As Jasper moved away from his screen door, Tim stood in the sun on the porch. He couldn't remember what he'd come to ask in the first place. The dull pain in his forearm wasn't coming from his hand. He had the odd feeling that his daughter was hiding in a tree trunk and crying for him to find her.

What he then said through the screen door surprised him more than anything all day had surprised him. He said, "You won't find another friend like Mars, Jasper. Not even for twenty bucks an hour."

The Resolution of Nothing

ELI'S FATHER CARRIES TWO THREE-BY-FOUR SHEETS of pegboard from the trunk of his Beetle up the front walk and around to the side door. He steps carefully over a pool of mud and the dusty termite planks that have been yanked from the porch and lie scattered on the yard. He almost knocks over the cardboard placard that reads "McGovern '72." (It's the second sign the family put up, since a neighbor set fire to the first.) Dangling from one of his hands is a plastic bag of hardware, shiny brass hinges and hooks. He reminds Eli to get the construction paper and the packet of corner tabs from the back seat of the car. Eli thinks, I'm glad to do something. It's my science project after all.

"Do you want to mount the photos on black paper or on the green?" Mr. Braunstein asks. He's sitting at his desk in the basement picking through a pile, squinting at his pencil notes on the backsides of the polaroids. He makes three stacks: pictures of jars with potting soil, jars with soil and three-week seedlings, and jars with soil and six-week bean plants. These stacks he divides again three times, the plants treated with the natural growth hormone, Auxin, the ones treated with Giberrellin, and the other ones, untreated. Eli knows that the last set are called the control group, but it doesn't make sense because those are the ones you don't try to control.

"I think the black paper looks better," Eli says.

"But the folder with your hypothesis, methodology and conclusion is black. Let's use the green," his father says.

"You're right, Dad. Since we bought the green, we might as

51

well use it." Eli laughs a nervous little hiccup.

"Where are my scissors?" his father says. "Were you playing with them?"

Fifth grade field trip Smithsonian Institute: Sister Joan wears the grey skirt and white turtle neck she wore for the Advent celebration when she played her guitar and sang, "Take Our Bread," with Brian Jarboe and Kim Connelly. That was last year, before Kim grew a lump in the front of her plaid uniform, before she was afraid to stand up straight in front of the room. That was before Jarboe got hung on the flagpole by the back of his underpants. One day you're a star, next day you're a turd—that's fifth grade, better behave yourself.

No uniforms today. The children receive extra white-lipped warnings before they charge out of the classroom to the bus. Earl looks the same as every morning in his lima bean green bus driver suit, except he's got no cigar. Eli likes Earl and usually gives him a high five at the top of the stairs. Earl keeps both hands on the wheel. Eli knows he's going to sit with Pat, Peabody, P The Man, but first he'll have to try all the seats. It's going to be summer soon and, God, he can't wait. He's wearing his flair jeans and his favorite red and purple striped T-shirt and no tie, of course, and no science packets today and you can forget about long division and all the rest. He feels like a solid turned liquid, like spreading out under the seat, expanding and expanding. I'll turn to gas, he thinks. I'll float out the window, but while I'm down here on the floor, I'll untie some shoes. Kim kicks and screams, "Stop it, you jerk!"

"Eli!"

Uh oh.

"Mr. Braunstein!" Sister Joan's face looks like her knee, which is only inches from Eli's nose, puffy and pink with pale blue highways. She reaches for his ear and puts her thumb in his eye instead. He cowers, elbows high in the air like he expects bombs to rain from heaven. She's stunned, and when he lowers his arms he can't say whether she's angry or sorry. It's best to look hurt for as long as I can, he thinks. He blinks his eye rapidly. "For someone who's supposed to be smart, you sure act like a fool sometimes." She says it without biting through her lip, like maybe she's not that angry, but it hurts more than the poke in the eye. I know exactly what she means, Eli thinks, I've heard it all my life.

Eli's older brother and sister got straight A's at St. Lawrence and both got scholarships to high schools on the side of town called Roland Park where the homes are made of fieldstone with pink and grey slate tops and soft green lawns and azalea bushes and those little round bushes his mother thinks are so cute called English Boxwoods. I'm just going to hold my eye, Sister Joan, and let you think about what you said. But she's not sorry, that's for sure. Sorry is the look she gets when she sings "Take Our Bread" or "Sons Of God," she looks like the first wet, wrinkled pancake you try to flip because you're too hungry to wait, but the face she's wearing now is the same she wore after she hit Donald Scott with a yardstick and told the class that wasting what God's given you is the biggest sin of all.

Father Bectal strolls up alongside the bus and pokes his head in the door. He says something to Earl who laughs and scratches his collar. Sister Joan swallows and then smiles like she's got it all under control. "This is a special opportunity," says Bectal. "A trip to the museum in Washington D.C." Sister Joan is wagging her head. It's bullshit, Eli wants to say, because I go to Washington D.C. every other weekend to visit my grandparents, and he does say as much with a curl of his lip to Peabody who already knows all about it. "I want to hear good reports from Sister Joan," Bectal says. He'd been standing with one foot on the lot and one foot on the bus's bottom step. He steps up and leans his head all the way in, "Mr. Braunstein, maybe you would stop by and see me when you all get back."

Eli's mother got Bectal's number the minute he showed up at

St. Lawrence. She said he isn't at all like Father Wilson, the former rector. Father Wilson left the parish for the Peace Corps, but when he gave a sermon it was like he was talking to you and the children flocked around him after mass. Mrs. Braunstein says Bectal's sermons are always about giving and he's always got one eye on the collection basket. "Besides," she says, "the man's got a nose like Nixon."

The Braunsteins have stopped going to church, except for the biggies, Christmas and Easter, and this year they skipped Easter. Mr. Braunstein never went anyway, being that he's Jewish, or he was raised Jewish. Once when Eli asked, his father said he doesn't know if there's a God. He said he wants to figure that out on his own. He said the evidence seems to be contradictory and inconclusive and when Eli's face puckered, he laughed and said don't worry so much about what I think. But Eli does worry. If there's no God, who's in charge? That's where Eli gets stuck.

Bectal's got two questions for Eli when he gets back. 1) Did you have a good time, Mr. Braunstein? And 2) Did you behave yourself? Eli almost says something he'd heard his father say to his mother: "The two are not mutually exclusive." He doesn't know what it means, only that it drove Mom out of the kitchen with her hands in her hair. If he liked Father Bectal, he'd tell him that the Hope Diamond was kind of a letdown, but the big pendulum that tells time was pretty cool, even though he couldn't touch it. He nods and says it was OK. Sister Joan was watching him extra close, but there's no reason to tell Bectal that.

"I want to ask you something else," he says. "What was the point of your science experiment?"

They are standing by a bench in the parking lot, halfway between the red brick square convent and the red brick square rectory. Eli hears the second bell which means that grades four, five and six march double-file to the lot in front of the brick rectangle school. He doesn't want Peabody to leave without him because there's something he wants to show Peabody in the cemetery on the way home—a new way to climb on top of the Finkley Mausoleum.

"You could read about it in my hypothesis," Eli tells him. He's careful to keep any flippancy out of his voice. Bectal sits on the bench and folds his arms.

"I read your hypothesis," he says. "I want you to explain it to me." There goes the third bell which means walk double-file down the hill to the crossing guard, but no one ever does that.

"What part didn't you understand?" Eli asks. He is trying to see around the side of the building, signal Peabody to wait.

"What I don't understand is how a boy who got a C- in Sister Miriam's class merited first prize in the Science Fair." Eli thinks he should be happy about the news, but his cheeks are getting hot and they always seem to know better.

"Tell me this," says Father Bectal, "what's an independent variable?" Suddenly Eli could tell him what an epiglottis is, that trap door at the top of the throat that tells you it's OK to swallow or not. He missed that one on Sister Miriam's last quiz.

"Maybe I have to look at my notes," Eli mumbles.

"Tell me where you got the idea for your science project."

"I guess I'd have to look at my notes for that one, too," he says. He scratches his nose to hide the nervous grin that sneaks across his lips.

"Well maybe you better do that." Father Bectal stands and unfolds his arms. "In the meantime, I'd like to have a talk with your father." He reaches in his pocket and hands Eli an envelope that's sealed. "Be sure to give him this when you get home."

When Eli reaches Gwynn Oak Boulevard, the eighth-grade crossing guards are already on the opposite side of the street and they've taken off their orange vests. That's fine, I can cross the street on my own for Christ sake. The walk through Lorraine

Cemetery is long and lonely. There's no point in scaling the ledges of the Finkley Mausoleum if there's no one there to watch. Maybe God is watching, but from what Eli has heard about God, He would not be favorably impressed. What would He think if Eli buried the envelope?

On the south slope, four headstones from the statue of the big brown buck on the granite pillar with the engraved letters B.P.O.E. where Eli once found a half-smoked butt wedged in the smooth stone, is a grave marked, Stocksdale. The girl Eli has had a crush on since the third grade Christmas party is named Jeannie Stocksdale. He wants to show her how he can do a backwards high jump over a three and a half foot hedge. She has dark brown hair and darker brown eyes like Marlo Thomas and sometimes she wears makeup but you can barely tell and she doesn't have breasts and she's not a good or bad student, except that often she gets in trouble for laughing at things that aren't funny. She's not one of the tough kids whose parents own taverns or garages behind the overpass on Windsor Mill Road. She's got her own mind, Eli thinks. She knows how to enjoy life. When he thinks about her, he gets a sensation that's like a fast elevator going down and like touching a sore when the scab gets brushed off. He wants to kiss her, but he feels silly and not at all like himself whenever he is near her, so he thinks he'll wait till the Valentine's Dance in seventh grade.

Eli has never told Peabody how he feels about Jeannie Stocksdale because he thinks that Peabody might feel the same way and he's not sure what effect such a discussion would have on their friendship. Today Eli can sit on the Stocksdale footstone and ponder his problems—he won't have to make any embarrassing acknowledgment about the coincidence of names or enter into a discussion about whether Jeannie is cool, or stupid like all the other girls. He chooses, after all, not to sit on the footstone, but on the grass beside it. And the choice, though he doesn't really understand it, reminds him of his question: should

I bury the envelope, and particularly the part about, is God watching?

The feeling Eli has next to the stone is like the feeling he got after his first confession, the big one before his first communion. He wanted to feel clean and ready. He had felt a lightness, not because his sins were so heavy, but because it had seemed so easy to let go of them. He'd had to try extra hard not to laugh when he told the part about blacking in the teeth on every man and woman in his sister's history book. When Eli sets down the envelope and combs his fingers through dandelion grass, a question occurs to him: If God knows all of my thoughts, why must I say my sins out loud? And then, God must know how I feel about Jeannie Stocksdale. The last thought troubles Eli because no one knows how he feels about Jeannie, but if he thinks hard, maybe there's a good side—maybe people go to confession because they really can keep secrets from God. He shivers, like after the first time he rode his bicycle down a flight of stairs. Then he sees one of the cemetery maintenance crew, the man with the double hairlip who keeps a six-pack of Pabst Blue Ribbon in the bushes and who chased Eli and Peabody when he saw them trying to climb onto the B.P.O.E. elk. Eli thinks, I better get my ass out of here—or that's how he will say it to Peabody when he sees him. Really he thinks, I sat down to think about a problem, and what I thought about was a whole universe of problems. Maybe that's my biggest problem, I can't think what I should think. In all of his thoughtfulness, Eli leaves the envelope sitting on the grass.

Daniel will not get home until dinner time because he is the editor of his high school's monthly newspaper, and this is, as he likes to say with a forced wink, "that time of the month." Beckie has field hockey practice after school. Mrs. Braunstein will pick them up in the Plymouth. Eli's mother just got a promotion at Maryland Family Services and she works late every day. She's not placing babies in people's homes any more, now she's teaching other ladies how to do it. She's super stressed all the time. Eli can sit on the porch and wait for them, but it's almost three hours and come on, as Beckie says, "that would be pathetic."

Eli's father is a lawyer. Once Peabody called him a "left wing lawyer" and Eli's best headlock couldn't get Peabody to say where he'd heard that one. Eli already knew that his Dad was not like lawyers he'd seen on TV. All of his clients are black and live in the poorest section of Baltimore. Is that what "left wing" means? That doesn't make any sense. His father owns two suits and both are shiny in the seat. Whatever kind of lawyer he is, he works all the time. He doesn't play. Twice he threw a football to Eli. Once the point of the ball hit Eli in a place called the solar plexus. When he finally finished crying his father was down in his cellar office typing. Once Daniel tried to tackle his father and he got a concussion. Mom says, "Your father doesn't know how to play," and that he's "too competitive." She has plenty to say about Mr. Braunstein. It's as if she fills blackboards and then she lets her breath out and tries to erase them, "because he's a good man," she says.

Eli is the only one home and after he checks the pantry and the dark space under his father's desk for murder hackers, he sits in his father's vinyl recliner with his father's headphones on listening to Dionne Warwick sing "Close To You." Sometimes the song injects color like fuel, like fuel injection into his day-dreams and lifts him out of his loneliness. He's never had a convincing picture of heaven, but he likes to think about the angels that "sprinkled moondust" in Jeannie Stocksdale's hair. Today, however, Eli's heart is so heavy it seems to be sitting on his stomach. This is the feeling that always comes with being "in trouble" and he wonders if Daniel or Beckie have ever felt it. He can't imagine when or why. He can't find the letter from Father Bectal and he has no idea what he'll say to his father. He presses his finger hard into the vinyl arm rest and prints the words: God

Help Me. He feels full of uncertainty. Why did I bring God into this? I'm not sure He's on my side. He tries to think purifying thoughts. He tries to feel sad for Jesus on the cross. Isn't this like a science experiment? He wouldn't really want God to know all of his thoughts. Once he imagined Sister Joan asking him to help her unclasp her bra for her bath and he felt such an ache in his trousers. He wouldn't want God to know about that. He thinks again about the epiglottis and then he tries to make his mind still. He waits.

From Peabody's backporch, Eli can see that his kitchen light is on. They're home. He is sliding Peabody's turtle around the perimeter of a cardboard box and he is about to tell his friend about the painted turtle he once saw in Woodlawn Creek, and then about something he'd heard about snappers and then he remembers a fact about how turtles lay their eggs, but it all seems so trivial. He'd like to talk to Peabody about his real problem, but they'd had an argument about politics and he suspects that Peabody is still angry and would take advantage.

Mr. Peabody is the head of the local Right to Life Committee and he'd shown his son some awful pictures and told him that McGovern wants to kill babies. Eli knew that couldn't be right, but he wasn't sure how to argue his point. He'd said something about Nixon and something about napalm because he'd seen some pictures too, but he wasn't able to put the pictures together in a way that made sense, not the way Daniel or his mother could do it. "I gotta go, Peabody," he says. He cuts across the back of the backyard, careful to cross the rock wall in the place where the ivy hasn't taken. Mom would appreciate the carefulness, but she'd never know about it. Maybe God is watching. Maybe God is not watching. He remembers something else he'd heard his father say: "You can't have it both ways."

The kitchen windows are steamy. He stops before the side door to hear what's being said inside. His father says, "Why don't *you* call Picker." He sounds angry. Picker is the man who is rebuilding the front porch, he seems to know something about how termites think. He is a very friendly black man who wears white overalls and can guzzle a whole bottle of water without taking a breath. Eli likes him, but he's heard his mother say that Picker is taking us for a ride. "I did call him," says Eli's mother. "I called him Monday. I called him Tuesday. You have responsibilities around here, too." Eli can't hear what follows over the sound of clanking pans and running water. He thinks, Mom and Dad could be talking about me. He'd overheard a similar conversation almost three months ago, Mrs. Braunstein urging Mr. Braunstein to get more involved in "your other boy's education." Eli's father's response: anger, silence, science project—some sudden brow-pinching curiosity about the effects of natural hormones on the growth of the stems, leaves, and roots of bean plants.

Eli hears his father call Daniel and Beckie from upstairs where presumably they've started their homework, then, "Where's Eli?"

"I'm here, Dad," Eli says, entering the kitchen from the top of the cellar stairs.

"Well, where've you been?" asks his father.

"Wash your hands," says his mother.

"I'm not too hungry," Eli says, but the words are absorbed in the steam and the sound of Beckie as she half-skips into the kitchen from the other doorway.

"It smells great, Mom," she says. "Hi Dad," she says. "Dad, guess what I got on the chemistry test."

Daniel pulls right up to the table. It's as if he never saw Eli. Ever since he started high school, he's been too damn busy to be a brother. Eli thinks again, I shouldn't say damn, even in my thoughts. "Dad, do you know how to spell legerdemain?" Daniel asks.

"That's a big word," Mr. Braunstein says. He winks at Eli's mother, "I know how to look it up in the dictionary."

"What is your article about, Daniel?" Mrs. Braunstein asks.

"Mom!" says Beckie. "Dad!"

"All right Beckie," Mrs. Braunstein says, "you'd better tell us."

"Guess!" Beckie says. She holds the bowl of rice pilaf just out of her father's reach.

"A hundred?" Mr. Braunstein reaches for the bowl as she pulls it farther away.

"You're close," she says.

"Ninety-eight."

"You're getting colder," Beckie says.

"So's the rice," says Mrs. Braunstein.

"I got a hundred and six, Dad, with the extra credit."

Mr. Braunstein raises a glass of water as if to make a toast. Daniel is watching his father as he spoons from a bowl onto his plate. Mrs. Braunstein instinctively stops Daniel from dropping peas on his placemat and she is smiling when her eyes settle upon her youngest blankly touching the prongs of his fork. "Tell us about your day, Eli," she says.

Mr. Braunstein still has his glass in the air. "What's the good news?" he rubs his knuckles on the top of Eli's head.

"Nothing, I guess."

"You had a field trip, right?" Eli's mother's smile turns to a mud mask on her face, like you could see little cracks where it started to dry. She can predict a wayward spoonful of peas, but she's clueless about the tears welling up in her second boy's eyes. And Eli is no less surprised. He'd been trying to make his mind empty, but it is impossible and he is exhausted. He can neither speak his thoughts nor hide his feelings, not really. *If I can't fool my parents, how can I ever expect to trick God?*

"I'm tired," he manages. He feels like there is a big, purple Advent candle stuck in his throat.

"You need something in your system," says Mr. Braunstein as he ladles rice onto Eli's plate.

"What is it, Sweetie?" says Eli's mother.

Daniel gives Eli a light punch on the shoulder. "Working too hard, old man?"

"Don't tease," says Mrs. Braunstein.

"We learned about something in biology," Beckie is all cheeks and cheerfulness. "E. Coli," she says. "It made me think of you."

"Don't tease Eli," says Mrs. Braunstein. "Don't."

Eli mumbles, "Excuse me," and walks out to the living room. He expects that in a minute his mother will come to comfort him. The heavy feeling that had begun with Father Bectal now drops him on his knees. He hugs a yellow and red checkered throw cushion. He'd been in trouble plenty of times and the feeling had never lasted longer than a runny nose, but this time it feels different. Many feelings feel different, but some feelings come and go, like the ache he gets in the crotch of his pants. Or like the thrill, the breathlessness he feels when he thinks about kissing Jeannie Stocksdale. Those feelings it seems he can bring on by using his imagination, but this heavy purple feeling, there's no getting away from it.

In the kitchen he can hear one chair scrape and then another, his father's voice saying, "I'll go." When he feels his father's warm hand making circles on his back, he doesn't know what will come out of his mouth, only that he needs to speak. The words are more evidence that he is not in control of his thoughts.

"What's up kiddo?" says Mr. Braunstein.

"Dad," Eli says, "maybe we could go to church together sometime."

The circles stop. "Why?" says Mr. Braunstein. "You can go to church whenever you like." His voice is unusually high, the way it gets when Mrs. Braunstein talks about sharing responsibilities.

Eli doesn't know what to say, or why he said what he said. He feels an odd sense of relief, though, as if he's not alone with his problem, and in fact he's not. His failure to answer Bectal's questions has implicated the entire family, made Daniel's achievements and Becky's achievements suspect. He's pulled his father down into his own badness. He still expects his mother will rescue him, but he doesn't know how it will happen. He thinks he might like to see his father get angry at Father Bectal. He'd like to see his dad get Bectal in a headlock, is what he'd really like to see. He'd like Father Bectal to see that his dad is not afraid of him or of his God. Or maybe he'd like to see that his dad is afraid of God. He's very confused. The only thing he feels sure of is that his father will not go to church. Mr. Braunstein wouldn't even go when Daniel asked him four years ago, when Daniel was afraid his father would be sent to hell. Eli remembers. He was only six then, but he felt the disruption of the household with Daniel's request and his father's refusal. It was worse than the discovery of termites in the rafters.

Eli tells his mother he doesn't have any homework because they'd had a field trip and the teachers forgot to give any. Really he should read the chapter about Manifest Destiny in his social studies reader, but Eli has trouble concentrating when he reads and both he and his mother know that he already has a lot on his mind. Together they watch "Petticoat Junction" and Eli's favorite, "Mannix." Joe rescues Peggy and her boy, Toby, from an old war buddy gone crazy. Eli's mother shares a can of caramel popcorn. For an hour and a half Eli forgets about Father Bectal, Jeannie Stocksdale and God. Mrs. Braunstein has been very short-tempered since she started her new job. She seems to be obsessed with what she calls "the clutter" in the house and the ugliness of Nixon, but for an hour and a half she mentions neither. Life is perfect until the screen fills with the names of the actors, photographers, musicians and Eli's mother says, "OK, it's time for bed."

Daniel is reading by a night-light in the bottom bunk when Eli enters the bedroom. He looks up and says, "Are you OK?"

"I guess so," says Eli. He climbs up onto the top bunk, squeals of springs and weak joints. "Do you ever think about hell?"

"God, what's up with you?"

"I won the science fair, Daniel."

"That's great. I don't get you at all. Didn't you tell Mom and Dad about it?"

"I'm in trouble. Or Dad's in trouble or something because Bectal knows I didn't do it."

Daniel closes his book and shuts off his light. He's fumbling with something in the dark. When he stops, Eli can almost hear him thinking. He'd won the science fair two years in a row and he'd gotten plenty of help from his father, but he'd also always gotten A's in science class. "Wilson was cool, but that guy is such a jerk," Daniel says.

"I know it."

"What are you going to tell Dad?"

"I don't know."

"You better tell him because he's going to find out sooner or later."

"Don't *you* tell him."

"All right."

"What would you do?"

"It would never happen to me." Daniel wears a brace at night to straighten his teeth, an elastic band that runs around the back of his neck and fastens onto a pair of tiny wire clamps on his upper plate. Eli hears the snap of the band and knows that the conversation is over. "I'd try to get some sleep," Daniel says. Within minutes Eli hears the soft staccato sniffle of air as it passes through his brother's nose.

He hears his father's slippers on the stairs and the creak of his parents' bed as he imagines his father sitting and unbuttoning his sweater. He stares at a glow-in-the-dark poster of the solar system on the wall above Daniel's desk. He hears his mother's meanest whisper, the one she uses to scold in the supermarket—it always gets everyone's attention.

"He's not lazy, he's different."

And then his father, who never whispers, "The others went

through it and they're fine."

"He's not fine."

"You want me to compromise—"

"Yes. And keep your voice down."

"Well he shouldn't be watching television, not on a school night."

"Ssshhh, would you."

It's Friday morning. Beckie has a field hockey game in the afternoon and she's having trouble finding her red bloomers. Daniel is pouring over the rough draft of his editorial. The announcement, "Breakfast is on the table," has been made three times. Eli hasn't moved, except to open his eyelids. He's not sure the solar system looks the way it looks on the poster and he wonders who and what it would take to convince him it is that way. Would it be enough if Dad said so? He has decided to be sick. It's the best idea he's had in a long time. He is practicing a suffering face when his mother comes into his bedroom. "I don't feel well," he says. And then, "I feel awful."

"What's the matter?"

"It's my throat." He does sound a little hoarse. It's easy if you don't sit up or brush your teeth.

Mrs. Braunstein palms his forehead and presses her fingers in at the sides of his neck. "It doesn't feel swollen," she says, "but there is something going around." She looks at her watch. "Oh Geez, I have an eight thirty."

"You better go Mom."

"I don't like to leave you here alone. Maybe you should come with me" She looks at her watch again and bites at one of her cuticles, "But I can't bring you with me."

"I'll be OK," Eli groans. "I just need a little rest." He drops his head back on the pillow, as if the exertion was all he could stand.

"You behave," says Mrs. Braunstein and Eli's brow wrinkles as she considers, "I mean, you get better, Sweetie."

Mrs. Braunstein hustles down the stairs and joins the others in the kitchen. Eli smells the familiar smells and hears the familiar sounds from the remove of his top bunk with nothing to look at but the sun and the nine planets. What would happen if one of the planets zipped out of its orbit into bigger outer space? Would the whole system fall apart? What's holding it all together? It's not easy to not think about God, he thinks. There had been some discussion in catechism about whether or not you keep your body when you go to heaven. Sister Miriam had one answer and Sister Joan had a different answer and Sister Joan wouldn't say which body, the one you happen to have when you die or the one you have in fifth grade or what. As hard as Eli tries he can't make a picture of heaven and he can't think of anything that would be fun for eternity. It isn't at all hard to think up hell.

He hears plates rattle and the thick sound of water pulsing through the dishwasher's rubber hose and then the heavy and light tread of feet down the cellar steps to the side door. "Where's Eli?" he hears his father say. He listens very hard to hear his mother's explanation, but he knows that his father's voice is the only one that carries through the house. He hears, "You're kidding!" And then, "Oh no!" The heaviest pair of feet thunders through the living room and up the stairs. He mumbles into his pillow: "Daniel's a damn fink." Mr. Braunstein pokes his head in. He needs to catch his breath before he can say, "Not feeling well?" Eli doesn't hear anger in his father's voice, only tenderness. It will take him all day and he still won't understand the feelings he's having at this moment. His throat is so constricted he can't speak. He nods. His father gives him a kiss on the forehead and says, "Well you better get better. We've got a date for Sunday."

Moments later Eli hears the wooden door close, the glass bang shut and his father's voice cheerful as spring, "Good morning, Mr. Picker. Glad to see you again"

The palms of Mr. Picker's hands are the color of canteloupe. Eli likes to watch the way he slings two by six planks up on his thigh, the way he takes up the heavy rotary saw and tosses the extension cord over his shoulder. Mr. Picker makes a few ear-piercing cuts, then wipes his brow with a dusty rag. "Surprised to see you around here, my friend," says Mr. Picker. "You must be sick, 'cause I know you wouldn't want to be missing school."

"Yea, I'm sick," Eli tries to get a rasp in his voice, but what he gets is a look at Mr. Picker's molars as he puts back his head and laughs.

"Well I guess we all of us need to take a day off sometime."

"I was wondering when you were coming back," Eli says.

"My mama had a stroke," Mr. Picker says. He makes another cut and brushes the edge of the board with his thumb. "I should be settin' with her, but I needs money now more 'n ever."

"I hope she's going to be OK," Eli says.

"I been saying my prayers."

"Do you go to church?"

"Nossir. I pray in my head. You don't need to go to church to talk to God. He can hear you fine wherever you are."

Eli wants to ask Mr. Picker some questions about heaven, and what exactly happens after we die, and what he thinks God looks like, but he doesn't know where to start. Picker is clearly very busy. He makes the same face that Eli's father makes when he is counting things you can't see, and if you interrupt Mr. Braunstein when he's making that face, he always gets mad. The sky is white and still and when the saw bites again, Eli goes back in the house. He thinks he will listen to a record, maybe American Pie, and he thinks he'll make some breakfast, maybe put a waffle in the toaster, and he thinks maybe staying home was a mistake. This in trouble feeling isn't ever going to go away.

On Saturday Eli plays Parcheesi at Peabody's house. Mr. Peabody is watching the news and something makes him angry.

He shouts at the boys to take their game outside and he shouts at one of Peabody's little sisters who bursts into tears and then he says something to Mrs. Peabody about "the dignity of the troops." When Eli suggests to his friend that they take the game over to his house, Peabody shakes his head. "I'm not allowed to go to your house," he says.

Sunday morning, ordinarily Mr. Braunstein enjoys his bagels, his pipe and three thick newspapers, *The New York Times*, *The Washington Post* and *The Baltimore Sun*. Ordinarily, he wears a pair of grey sweat pants and one of his striped polo shirts—his pajamas—until it is time to change, to pack the family in the Plymouth and visit his folks in D.C. or better still, not to change, simply to rise from his cellar summoned by the smell of pot roast and baked potatoes. Ordinarily, no invariably, he clips an article or two or three to share at the dinner table. Often these articles are inspirational accounts of someone who's been able to, as Eli's father would say, "make a difference," and almost always concerning "the plight of the poor." Eli can't understand his father's pleasure any more than Mr. Braunstein can appreciate his son's wonder on a Sunday morning stroll through the woods down to the creek where a crayfish might clamp down on the end of a muddy paper straw or later in the day, when Peabody gets home from church, they might find a jay's nest with some eggs in it.

He's a good man, Eli thinks, when he sees his father early Sunday morning in one of his worn suits. No, these are words like ticker tape that run through Eli's mind. He can't say if his father is a good man or not a good man. One day maybe I'll have my own mind, he thinks. He senses that his father is uncomfortable, the way he reaches for his briefcase, then sets it down, the way his tongue presses the inside of his cheek like maybe he has a toothache. "This is how your father tells you he cares about you," his mother had told him. "He did the same for me once years ago."

Eli thinks, when they sit side by side in the bubble which is his father's car, I asked for this. And then he thinks, Oh shit (shoot), what in the hell (heck) did I expect?

"Listen," Mr. Braunstein exhales. His hand hovers over the ball of the stick shift before he pulls out of first gear, "I don't know if there is a God, but I know I don't believe that God had a son named Jesus. I believe there was a man named Jesus who had some good messages for all of us." No, Eli decides, I can't let Dad speak to Bectal, I just can't. Mr. Braunstein is driving too fast now for second gear, the engine wants to explode, the handle of the glove compartment is vibrating. "You don't have to believe what I believe. You can believe whatever you want. But I think you have a right to know what I think. That's what this is about, isn't it?"

Eli nods. Is that what this is about? He'd thought it was about a C- and a science project, or about acting silly on a field trip. This is much too big. He can feel his father looking at him like glaring sun on the side of his face. "I mean," Mr. Braunstein says, "if you really knew what I thought, it would probably seem absurdly strange to you." Eli is afraid that his father will continue and though under other circumstances he thinks he'd like very much to understand what his father believes, right now he doesn't want to hear anything that is absurdly strange. Mr. Braunstein continues, "What I think is that each of us creates God, and not the other way around. We do it in our thoughts and our words and our actions. We rely on our gods to make us feel safe and cared for" He exhales again and finally shifts into a higher gear. He pats Eli on the knee. "After we do this church thing, you and I can go over to the IHOP and get a nice breakfast." Eli had always liked the six kinds of syrup on the tables at IHOP, but this morning he can't imagine eating.

As they walk through the lot toward the big white double doors of the church, Eli sees Mr. Peabody's brown Nova. Mr. Peabody is an usher for the early morning mass. Eli knows that his father suspects Mr. Peabody of having set fire to the family's first McGovern sign. He is not sure how he wants his father to feel about this church outing, but he thinks that this is a bad way to start. Nonetheless, Eli has seen no hesitancy in his father's stride or on his face, to the contrary, an odd springiness and an odder smile like Hey, won't this be fun? Hadn't it been this way with the science project, too? After a period of brooding and deliberation, it was Mr. Braunstein's style to plunge in. He claps Eli on the shoulder and picks up the pace. "Do you know," he laughs, "the last time I set foot in a church, I came out a married man."

They enter a pew midway down the center aisle. Eli sees a few of his classmates with their parents, but none that he likes. He looks for Jeannie Stocksdale, but he doesn't see her. Everyone happens to be sitting and so Eli and his father sit. It feels funny. In front of the Tabernacle, beneath the big wooden crucifix, Father Bectal gestures with his palms open at his sides, "All rise." All the parishioners, including Mr. Braunstein and his son, stand and when Eli cautions a glance, he sees that his father still has a grin on his face. It is not clear to Eli whether his father thinks being in church is funny. But Eli thinks it's funny. It's not funny. He doesn't want to laugh, but it suddenly seems like a game of Simon Says. "Please be seated."

Bectal wears a white lacy outfit that touches the tips of his black shoes. It's not funny. Bectal's sermon is about the time Jesus scolded the Pharisees for excluding children from the spiritual lessons. What's most not funny about this is that though it's been four months since Eli sat through a Sunday mass it was the same scriptural reading and the same commentary the last time. Eli watches Bectal's eyes, just as his mother had described, following the collection basket in Mr. Peabody's hands. It's not funny.

Here comes Mr. Peabody slowly up the center aisle, waiting with his hands folded at his waist. When he sees Eli and Mr. Braunstein he gives the slightest dip of his chin, a recognition that is not quite recognition, nor is it quite Mr. Peabody as Eli has so often seen him. It is not the man who called Muhamed Ali an "uppity nigger." It is not the Mr. Peabody who swats at his children like flies. This is a funny game, a funny game, and what would God think if He could read my thoughts, and here in His own house? Eli wonders if these are his thoughts, or if somehow miraculously he is seeing the mass through his father's eyes. Absurdly strange. He tries to make his mind blank and as usual he cannot. He feels panic and he looks up at the rafters to steady himself, but it makes him dizzy. He hears small hard shoes on the tile floor and looks back at Jeannie Stocksdale settling in two rows behind him. She winks and presses a hymn book against her lips to prevent herself from laughing. Eli erupts before he can push the sleeve of his jacket into his mouth. Mr. Braunstein takes the sound to be a sneeze and with that same odd grin he turns and says, "Bless you."

"All be seated," Bectal says, but all heads turn. Eli's sobbing laughter sends a tremor through the crowd. Some must think he is possessed, doubling over, then falling backwards, then curling like an infant on the bench until his father takes him by the arm. There is a brief pause in the proceedings while Mr. Peabody ushers Mr. Braunstein and Eli out of the church.

Eli's father is twenty steps ahead fumbling at unlocking the car. He is confused, maybe, embarrassed, maybe. He is speechless. Father Bectal is twenty yards behind dipping a wafer into a chalice, speaking the words of transformation. Nothing is resolved. Eli is in more trouble now than ever, but he stops and stands in the center of the small square courtyard of St. Lawrence Church, in a brand new relation to God. He feels lighter than he did after his first confession. Then he'd only let go of his sins. He closes his eyes and composes the prayer of his lifetime: "Wish Me Luck."

The Full Six

"I CHALLENGE YOU TO GET A STRAIGHT ANSWER from Pop," Nick says, pulling on a toasted bagel, a dab of cream cheese in his sandy beard.

"What are you talking about?"

"Ask him anything you want. I challenge you." I can hear Pop stepping down the stairs from his bedroom, slippers now scuffling across the living room floor.

"One straight answer?"

"One."

"How long?" Nick is bare-chested in his boxers, beachballs in rainbow colors. He grabs my wrist and wipes my flannel sleeve across his mouth.

"You jack-off." I fake a quick jab to his hairy belly, but he doesn't flinch.

"I'm a jack-off?" he says. "So then you're getting some, I presume." I shrug. "I'll give you till noon. Three hours."

"What for?"

"Ten big ones?"

"I guess you don't need money at college," I say.

"Good morning, Pop," Nick says. With one hand Pop holds together his terry cloth robe and with the other he pulls a carton of two percent from the fridge. His hair is the color of Nick's, the color of sand in the sun, but he keeps it wet and combed back to cover the thin spot on top.

"What's good about it?" he grunts. Nick wipes his hand over my bald head—something that no one can seem to resist doing since I shaved off my red curls.

"Twenty," Nick says.

"You're on," I say. "Did you sleep well, Pop?"

"Who wants to know?" Pop says. Nick's tongue smooths over his front teeth.

"Doo, here," he squeezes my skull like he's palming a basketball and he turns my face toward Pop, "needs something to keep his head from sliding off the pillow."

"Power sander," Pop says. "That'll take the shine off, Dru, whadya say?"

Doo is Nick's little twist on Dru, short for hairdo. He tagged me the first moment he saw me, when he and Pop returned from the airport and were walking up the front walk from the car. Maybe Pop had told him I'd shaved my head and so Nick had time to think up a name. I don't know what those two talk about when they're together.

Nick had a Nike sports bag, a duffle and a pair of roller blades slung over his shoulder. Pop had the *Sunday Sun* and *The Washington Post* tucked under his arm. The walk was ice dusted with a layer of snow. Nick took it right, like Nick, like it was nothing out of the ordinary. And Pop took it pretty cool for a man of fifty-five. He wasn't walking sideways or taking tiny steps, but I could see he was worried about falling. He tries hard to hide it— the fear of falling look—the quick glance downward without lowering the chin thing. He tries extra hard on the holidays when Nick comes to visit.

I'm eyeing the bagels but I can't touch them. The Christmas tourney is in two days and I have to drop five pounds to make one-forty-seven. Kick some ass in the Christmas tourney and I'll get a good seed in the MSA's—the Maryland Scholastic Association's wrestling finals. If I don't drop the five, I'll be facing Louie Ciapparelli in round one. Fucked. Chip wears a safety pin in his warm-up jacket for every guy he's decked during the season. Thirteen matches, so far. Thirteen pins.

I want to think up some questions to put to Pop, but the first thing I have to do is get my ass out of the kitchen. I take a six of diet RC colas from the pantry and stuff them into the refrigerator. I don't see the lasagna in the Corning Ware. I don't see the Lemon Meringue pie.

"I'm going running."

Nick shoots a look at the clock above the fridge. His lips make the shape of *twenty*.

"No shit."

"That's not the way you talk at your mother's house." Pop's voice is flat, bored.

"How would you know, Pop?" I don't wait for an answer. He doesn't have an answer. I walk back to the den, my bedroom when I stay at Pop's. He cleared one long shelf of his law books so I have a place to keep my clothes. I used to come every weekend, then every other weekend. In the past few months I've only visited Pop when I think Mom wants to get me out of the house. "Why don't you go look after your father," she says. "Go keep him company." He never said that he wanted my company, or that he didn't. We don't talk much. He used to ask me about wrestling, but when I'd tell him about Granby Rolls, Toe-picks, Duck-unders, whatever, he'd get a blank look, start taking dishes out of the dish rack. Once he said, "I don't understand why you kids would want to starve yourselves like that."

I dig a pair of Converse high-tops out of my red and gold Cardinal Gleason sports bag. Converse are not good running shoes, they suck, but I need high-tops to make my ankle weights fit snug on my ankles.

Marycat, Nick's girlfriend when he comes home to visit— "the local squeeze," he calls her—said that she heard that ankle weights can fuck up your knees. No, she said ankle weights can *be harmful* to your knees. She looked so sincere when she said it, like someone trying on a new hat in a mirror. Nick and I had heard Mom say exactly the same thing. Maybe Oprah had a special on knees, who knows. The weirdest part, though, was that Nick didn't gurgle in his beer or shoot me a sideways grin; he nodded his head real serious like Pop used to when Pop could still hold one of those things called a conversation. There's a lot of Pop in Nick. The fact that Nick's living three thousand miles away in sunny Santa Cruz only seems to have made more of the Pop in him come out.

The more it is you try to get away from a thing or a person, the more it is that the thing or person will take over your life. That's my theory. It's rough, still. It comes to me when I'm jogging through slush puddles in the parking lot of Woodlawn Mall. My thighs feel like hot bags of sand as I chug on past Pargo's, Red Lobster and a nameless, little, beige building that I figure is about half-way. Every time I reach that building I have the same couple of thoughts. I think, good, I'm about half-way. Or if my legs are really burning, I think, oh shit, I'm only half way. I hope I never have to work in a building like that. If I had to spend my days there, I'd be afraid I'd disappear. And I always leap to thinking about Pop; how he used to be right in the center of things, high profile. Him and Mom.

They had friends at the house all the time. I must have heard a hundred stories about the days when Pop dominated the football and lacrosse fields around Maryland and Virginia—Mr. Tidewater Regional Whatever. He was a force to be dealt with back then. People still recognize his name once in a while. But you'd never know he was a superstar by looking at him, not anymore. It's like he was under the big lights, in the center of the circle of the wrestling mat is how I see it, but then he got beaten and crawled off under the bleachers and out of sight.

On past the beige building, past the thoughts that make me tired, Dino's Chevrolet, Burnside Field, Lorraine Cemetery, and up and down to the old stadium to climb the stairs, to feel my lungs get raw, to bust it because I don't want to be anonymous. If I can stay undefeated until the MSA's, even Louie Ciapparelli will know my name.

Pop and Nick are watching a football game on Pop's new twenty-six inch Sony when I get back. A zebra blows his whistle and swings his arm in a full circle and another sets the ball on the hashmarks. "College or pro?" I ask from the doorway, picking snow out of the laces of my sneakers.

Nick waits. Pop picks up The Living Section of *The Sun*. He doesn't seem to hear me.

"Niners and Colts," Nick says.

"Man that pisses me off," I say. The newspaper rattles. "Why'd the Colts leave Baltimore, Pop?" I ask. He folds down a corner of his paper and looks at Nick.

"Why does anyone leave Baltimore? Ask your brother."

"I sure as hell wouldn't go to Indianapolis," Nick says. I have a Hefty bag on under my sweat shirt to help me lose water weight but I can't stand the feeling of it sticking to my back. I start up the stairs for a quick, hot shower.

"No, Pop, how come?" He folds down his paper again and says, "Because." I'm going to use the twenty bucks to get a new set of dumbells. "Because you need a shower," he says. He winks at Nick.

Nick has his bare feet up on an ottoman. He curls and uncurls his tan toes. Does he think he's still at the beach? It's only ten thirty. I have plenty of time. Shower. Suck down a diet cola. Think. But it's starting to bug the shit out of me. I sure don't need Nick to prove that Pop's gotten impossible to talk to. I know that better than anyone.

It was three-and-a-half years ago when our happy little household turned into the Nightmare on Poplar Drive. Mom found out about Pop's little extracurricular action, "the law student without the briefs," she called her, and our dinners got stone quiet and our desserts exploded in shattered dishes. The week after

Nick left for college one of the neighbors called the cops. I remember Mom crying over a cup of coffee, Pop standing on the front porch making a joke with the police officer who happened to be the son of his law partner. They shook hands and laughed, but it took forever for the cop to drive off, and even after he was gone I could still see shadows from his cherry-top flickering through our house. Nick never saw that.

At Cardinal Gleason, Nick could get any babe he wanted. He was Superjock and he never even had to work at it. The lacrosse coach called him Hat Trick Nick. His stickwork was awesome, left hand just as strong as his right. He played attack and there wasn't a defenseman in the MSA that could touch him. He'd be high-stepping around the crease, pump, pivot, cradle left and right, plant a foot, throw back his head, lurch forward till the dude with the long stick couldn't do anything but shit in his pants, then Nick'd quick double-back, fake high and bounce low or fake low and whip the little sucker up in the corner of the goal. I remember once a goalie throwing down his stick and shaking off his gloves, the Cardinal Gleason red and gold pom-poms waving wildly, cowbells clanging, and feet stomping on wooden benches. Nick was as cool as could be, hunched over studying his shoelaces. That was early in the Spring, four years ago, still a little chill in the air. Mom and Pop were sitting on the top row of the bleachers with their red and gold wool blanket stretched across their knees.

Last week I drove Mom and Roger out to BWI to catch a charter flight to Fort Lauderdale. Roger is the man that Mom is seeing. Nick calls him Roger the Garager because he owns one of those Self-Storage places out on the edge of Reisterstown. He's OK with me. As far as I can tell he's got nothing to say, but it's better that way. Mom clings onto him tight. That's OK, too. You can tell he cares about her the way he carries her bags, and the way he takes her hand when they come to a slippery sidewalk. He's a real old-fashioned gentleman kind of guy.

Roger got out of the backseat and opened the trunk. He lifted out a leather suitcase and draped a matching valise over his arm. Mom opened her door but didn't get out. She put her cold hand on my cheek.

"Tell Nick I'm sorry I'll miss him this visit." She dipped into her purse and fingered for her airline tickets, then reached back and brushed my cheek again. Her hand rode under my Gleason's cap and smoothed up the back of my head, until I jerked my shoulders a little and she pulled back. "And I want you to give your brother a big hug and a kiss for me."

"Yeah. Right." When I looked at her I saw that her eyes were puddling up. Maybe from the blast of cold air.

"You boys are just like your father," she said.

"I can't park here, Mom," I said. She's as bad as Pop in her way. If she doesn't want to hear you, she doesn't hear you.

"You know your father was pretty hot with a lacrosse stick in his day."

"I know."

"Of course the game was different back then. The sticks were made of wood and leather and catgut, not like the plastic things kids use now. A lot of things were different."

"I know."

"But your father was just like Nick, cool as can be."

"Think you'll see any reindeer down in Lauderdale?" I said.

The trunk finally slammed shut and Roger bent at Mom's door. I was eager to get to the gym so I could do some upside-down push-ups in the sauna.

"You know," she said, "he never even said he was sorry." Her tears were real. I was trying hard to swallow.

"I can't park here, Mom."

"Maybe you're different, Dru. You're so intense."

"Yeah," I said. "Well, you and The Dodger have a good Christmas."

"Don't make fun of him," she said. "Not you." She touched

her knuckles once more on my cheek, this time warm and moist from having wiped her eyes.

The Christmas tourney is being hosted at MacDougal High this year. MacDougal has a couple of decent grapplers, but it's like they don't have any heart. Rich kid prep schools bug the shit out of me. MacDougal has a yellow-haired guy named Seamus in the one-hundred-fifty-seven pound class who I beat with an ankle pick in O.T. He knows more moves than I do, but I beat him because I wore his ass out. At one-thirty-seven they have a little muscle-head named Rodriguez. Judging from all the posters around the gym, some people seem to think he might give Chip's little brother, Rico, a match. The Ciapparelli's have a goddamn mat in their basement. Mr. Chip was olympic. Rodriguez might go the full six, I thought, but more likely he'd get decked in the first period.

Nick and Marycat drop me off and head down Reisterstown Road to Roy Rogers for fried chicken. They promise they'll have three double cheeseburgers for me for after the weigh-ins. Pop doesn't come. He said he had a couple of letters to write, things he'd been sitting on too long. It seemed strange to me, but I just let it go. I thought he was pissed off at me. Who knows? He wouldn't have said so if he was.

A pudgy kid, team manager with a lime-green necktie and lime-green blazer, checks his clipboard and leads us with a wave to our row in the locker room. Red and gold magic marker letters spell out Cardinal Gleason on a slip of white posterboard. The locker room smells like talcum powder and pine trees. Ours always smells like someone just finished taking a squirt on the heater.

Coach Kerrow tells us to relax and get ready for weigh-ins. He is one hundred percent Gleason, a flannel shirt rolled up at the sleeves and a plaid tie. When he's not coaching he's hauling housing panels for the lumber supply in Towson. He doesn't know shit about wrestling, but he knows how to whip our asses into shape. Whitcomb, our one-eighty-seven is holding his belly and groaning. He chewed a handful of Ex-Lax last night to help bring his weight down. Coach Kerrow hands me a set of nail clippers.

"Pass them around, Dru. I'm going to check the seeding chart."

He winks at Whitcomb. "Better get back on the pot, kid." He snaps his finger on my head just above my ear. "I got to say, you're looking scary, Dru."

"Good," I say. "Let 'em tremble." I punched Orbo, our one-fifty-seven, hard on the shoulder, "Hey, stay loose man. You've got nothing to lose."

Kerrow takes forever. Our nails are clipped and we're stripped down to our jock straps waiting for our call to weigh in. Orbo head-butts a locker and screams in his deepest lung ripping holler "LET'S KICK SOME A. CARDINAL GLEASON."

"Where the fuck is the coach?" the lightweight says. I sit on the bench and watch my toes flex. After our heavyweight's bare ass waddles by my face for the third time I stick my foot against a locker and block his passage. "Save your strength."

A door to the gym swings open briefly and we can hear MacDougal's brass band trip into "We Are The Champions." Pop might still show up. I expect to spot Marycat's red and gold sweater up on the top row and see Nick and Pop sitting on opposite sides of her. I want to show him what I can do—what he could do if he put his heart into it.

Kerrow walks right past our row of lockers like he's lost.

"Coach," I call out. He digs his hands into the back pockets of his khakis. He pulls them out. He loosens his tie and then he tightens it back up.

"Orbo," he says, "I've got good news for you." Orbo slams his head into the locker again and screams. "Settle down," Coach says. "Dru, don't freak."

He doesn't have to say anymore. Chip dropped weight too. Of

course he'd drop to one-forty-seven with the Nationals coming up next week. Fuck. I'm fucked. The coach says something I can't hear and then he rubs my head. Green blazer waddles up and points us to the scale.

"Your turn, Cardinal Gleason," he says.

I was decked once, my first varsity match. Nothing sucks worse. It's like getting trapped in a burning house. First you're fighting for air, then you're melted down into a useless puddle. After you burn to death though, you don't have to look anybody in the face. I have no chance of beating Chip, but I sure as hell don't want to give him another saftey pin to wear in his warm-up jacket.

Kerrow doesn't seem to think I look so scary anymore. He tilts his head and gives me a long, slow look. "You got nothing to lose out there, Dru." He must have been thinking just what I was thinking two days ago when I started pumping Pop with hard questions: Man, I'm glad I'm not you.

"What are you going to do this afternoon?" I asked. He put *The Sun* down beside him and picked up *The Washington Post*.

"You do something," he said. "I'll sit here and read about it in the paper."

"That's it?" I said. Nick stroked his beard to hide his grin.

"What's this, Twenty Questions?" Pop said.

"Let's go out and toss a ball around. Let's see if you've still got that arm," I said. I thought I saw a flicker in Pop's eyes, like there was nothing in the world that he wanted to do more than throw a couple crisp spirals to me and Nick.

"All I've got left is curveballs, Kiddo," he said. Nick raised his eyebrows and touched a finger against the back of his bare wrist.

"No shit." I could feel heat in my face. The three hours had passed. It wasn't about the fucking twenty, though. Goddamn Nick. I was standing on the stairs and I squeezed the rail of the banister so hard the wood creaked. "Did you just stop loving Mom, Pop?" I said. The paper rattled. "Did you just give up?" It was a minute after noon. He didn't say anything.

The brass band kicks in again, "We Are The Champions, My Friend. We'll Go On Fighting Till The End," as Rodriguez stands up from his team's bench. He rolls his head in a circle around his tree stump neck. A teammate picks him up from behind, hands locked under Rodriguez's thick elbows, twists him and shakes him until his back cracks. MacDougal's coach, lime-green tie and all the rest, pulls Rodriguez by his headgear and shouts something in his ear. I can't hear what he says because of the brass and the footstomping and because of my pulse. The coach gives Rodriguez a quick slap on the chin and tries for another across the buttcheeks but Rodriguez has already charged to his edge of the circle.

Rico. Little Chip. Little son of a bitch. Watching him do his thing gets me double-freaked. It starts at the handshake. Rodriguez walks to the center and a step beyond like he's walking through concrete, traps and lats tweaking like guitar strings. Little Chip takes one step forward, if that. He doesn't shake. He taps his knuckles against the back of Rodriguez's hand.

Does muscle-head go the full six? He doesn't last twenty-five seconds. He tries to tie up head and shoulders with Rico, but Rico ducks under and pops up behind, easy as a square-dance, like something both partners had agreed on. It's nothing fancy, but Rodriguez is suddenly frantic. Little Chip sets a simple pick behind his heel and lowers him down onto the mat. From there he slides up and hooks his right arm, cranks it good and hard. Rodriguez, the poor son of a bitch, reaches back. Never, never, never reach back. Kerrow doesn't have much to teach us, but he taught us that.

Little Chip doubles him up with a chicken wing—the poor sucker's elbows are like welded together behind his back—and then he walks it over smooth as cake. Rodriguez's neck folds until one, two shoulders touch the mat. Slam, whistle, thank you, ma'am. A tuba player put his lips to the aperture and prepares to blow until a green blazer slices the air for silence.

Seems like all the air has been sucked out of the gym.

I spot Nick and Marycat across the floor in the second row. She holds up a white paper bag, my double cheeseburgers. If neither of the two monkeys before me decides to roll over and read the watts on the ceiling bulbs, then I have just under six minutes before facing off with Big Chip. I can't even swallow my own spit.

Nick crosses the gym floor with Marycat skipping at his heels. He puts an envelope down beside me and she sets the bag of double cheeseburgers on top of it.

"Do it to 'im Doo," he says. Marycat giggles.

"You're the best, Dru, Honey." She kisses her fingers and touches my bald head.

There's a slap and a whistle and oh shit. One of the monkeys before me got himself caught in a reverse cradle. Way off in the far corner someone shakes a pair of purple pom-poms. Coach Kerrow calls, "Dru." He squeezes my biceps but he doesn't slap my chin. Instead he gives me a slow, sorry-looking smile—just like Mom did before she got out of the car at the airport. I don't know whether I want to hug him or punch his lights out. I must look terrified.

I've never gotten a letter from Pop before. Why would he write? Mom's house is only a twenty minute drive across town, a simple phone call, but he never called. Pop never just dropped by. Maybe he doesn't want to run into Roger, I don't know. Weekends together have gotten so strange, so lonely.

"You don't want to spend your time with an old man," he once said. "Whadya want to do kid, feed the ducks with me, or go out and get laid?" Maybe I should have said, "Feed the ducks." Maybe I should have hit him with a Soufflé, a Pancake, a Double Chicken-wing, a Reverse Half-nelson, a Fireman's Carry, something to keep him on the mat, in the center where he belongs. Mom didn't stop loving. She didn't give up.

Big Chip doesn't juke around. He stands on his rim of the circle like his little brother did, looking bored. I walk out slow because my knees ache. When the ref jerks his hand up signaling the start, I see the mat ripple up like a wave between us and for the minutes that follow I feel like I'm tumbling in a rip-tide; rolled, battered, and breathless. I think I have my eyes closed through the entire first period. All I can hear is my heart.

I get the whistle twice for stalling. Chip turns me on my back four times. Two times the buzzer goes off just before the ref is about to slap the mat. I crawl out of the circle five times. Once I even drag Big Chip right up to Nick and Marycat's feet. I'm so hungry and scared and tired, a couple of times I think about giving in to get it over with.

Big Chip wins twenty four to one. He got five takedowns, four near-falls, one reversal and two penalty points. I got one escape. He shakes his head with disgust while the ref grabs his right hand and lifts it in the air. He says, "I'll be seein' ya in the MSA's."

I have exactly enough strength to walk to the locker room and peel off one sweaty sock. I sit on a bench and stare at nothing for almost half an hour. Nick sits with me for a minute.

"Fucking cheer up," he says, "You're the only guy he didn't deck all year. You probably ruined his Christmas."

"Yea."

"You got to learn to lighten up, Dru. How you ever going to get yourself a squeeze if you're so damned uptight?"

"Yea."

"Eat your cheeseburgers. Me and Marycat'll be in the car." He leaves me alone with the bag and the letter. I tear the envelope and find two tens paper-clipped to a half sheet of paper.

Dear Dru,

This twenty dollars belongs to you. The gag was Nick's idea. It wasn't fair. I'm sorry. The answer to your question is no. I didn't know I loved your mother until now.

Sure, Pop and Nick have always been alike. Always cool. They make what they're doing look easy. They like their gags, I guess, because sometimes they get bored. With all my strength I peel off the other sweaty sock, then sit and stare some more.

Me and Pop, now we've got something in common. We get so hungry sometimes, so hungry, it's like we can't eat.

Gauge

I'M EYEING THE TEMPERATURE GAUGE. I expect my car to overheat. The red needle holds in place a quarter inch above the C. Do I want the car to overheat? I don't think so.

First stop, drop off a story written by a student at Berkeley Junior. I'm happy to share my comments. I liked the story. Second, a job interview in Marin at a group home for developmentally disabled adolescents. Third, down to Palo Alto for my ex-girlfriend's dance recital. I'm watching the gauge. If the needle is going to move, I want to see it move. I want to move it with my eyes. I don't want any surprises.

I squirted water into the radiator at Chevron this morning. Tell me about estrangement. "Baby, baby, where did our love go?" Diana Ross wants to know. My question, I think, is simpler. Do I want the car to overheat? I don't, but if the heat's rising I want to see it.

We were engaged, the dancer and I. She's in medical school and she dances. She does what she sets her mind to do. She does it, grinding like the gears of a machine, she gets it done. Could use a little oil, I guess, or grace, like the nuns in my elementary school used to say, but she's efficient.

I wish I could take back the comments I made on the girl's story. It wasn't very good really, but she took some risks. One way of seeing stories is as a succession of problems to be solved. The storyteller creates a problem, then solves it. Or doesn't solve it. Some problems are more interesting than others. The girl's solutions were too neat for me. Her solutions were creative, but too sensible, too neat. She's young though.

My girlfriend—ex, cut me out cold. I saw it. I saw the needle dropping. But so cold and so sudden, white steam. She turned cold and I turned mad. I was watching, but some things I didn't see coming. Like the bolt under the vinyl ceiling of my Datsun. I've taken to punching the ceiling when I get mad, but I didn't expect to tear a gash in my knuckle. I didn't expect to greet my ex-girlfriend with blood on my hand.

The job in Marin was for a counselor in a group home. Erik, a smartly dressed man with a pony tail, interviewed three of us— Genna, Kerry, and myself—around a large oak table. He spoke slowly and gave the appearance of listening, punctuating the conversation with occasional slow, grand gestures. He opened the dining room curtain and revealed a pair of fig trees and three rhododendron bushes in full bloom. Erik exhaled as if the beauty caught him by surprise.

He described a resident named William. Erik said William is a handful, manic-depressive, but that on good days William could charm birds out of the trees. Genna nodded as if she knew William, as if she'd seen the birds coming out of the trees. Kerry lit up with a giggle. I asked Erik who was paying for this beautiful home in beautiful Marin, who could live here and who could not, and his smile receded. It looked like a movie star smile, all lips.

Erik gave me a convoluted explanation, but I have no reason to doubt it. There are state funds, city and county funds, MediCal and Golden Gate Regional Facility funds; and when he said Golden Gate I wondered if my car would overheat on the bridge. I wondered how I'd handle myself at the dance recital. I'd try to stay cool—give this friendship thing a chance.

Genna said she'd been working at a one-hundred-fifty bed homeless shelter in the Tenderloin and that she wanted the job in Marin because she needed relief. It had depressed her, getting involved in the lives of people who are so self-destructive. She cared for them all, but she couldn't take it anymore.

My ex told me that she couldn't stand the smell of cigarettes on my clothing, the smell of wine on my breath. Why hadn't I gotten the car fixed. She said she wants more out of life than I do. Genna said that besides the burnout, she thought the mayor was going to cut funds to the shelter. She shrugged and said she was looking out for herself and then she looked around the table at each one of us.

The eighth grader's story was based on an assignment I'd given to the entire class. I'd asked the kids to put themselves in the double-laced hightops of a boy named James. James is sixteen and he loves basketball. He wants to try out for the team, but practice times conflict with his paper route. In the scenario I created, James' mother, Marilyn, had recently lost her job playing saxophone in a night club. The family was facing hard times. In short, I gave the kids a couple of characters and a problem. That's where fiction begins, I think. Why it is that people are drawn in by other people's problems is a bit of a mystery—as if we don't have enough problems of our own.

Erik tilted his head and asked Kerry what she saw herself doing in five, ten years. "I'm not exactly sure," said Kerry, tilting her head complementary to the angle of Erik's, "but I guess I want to be working with disabled people in some way. I have always been drawn to disabled people, since I was a little girl. It just gives me a good feeling." Erik turned his body in his chair without bending his neck and put the same question to Genna and then to me. "Ten years," I said, "I don't know. I hope I'm not looking for a job in ten years." Erik laughed and made a remark about the importance of humor and Genna nodded.

My ex and I had been engaged, but with like a pull on the throttle or a step on the clutch, we became disengaged. Released, I guess is how she sees it. For me it's more like losing grip, spinning but never catching. Most of the eighth graders at Berkeley Junior solved James' problem. Simple. James gives up his paper route. Marilyn finds another job in another night club. Basketballs neatly swishing through hoops. Or James is so good that the basketball coach does not require him to practice. Or, as the girl's story had it, James called the man who supervised newspaper deliveries in his neighborhood, a Mr. Clyde Parker, and the two agreed upon a time when James could deliver papers which did not conflict with basketball practice. Problem solved.

But what I liked about her story, what made it different from the others, is that the girl wanted something else. Maybe she wanted *more out of life* to borrow the phrase from my ex. She solved the problem, I suppose, because that's how stories are supposed to end—not ten years from now still looking for a job, or ten years still spinning; but successful, complete, or even dead, tragic. Obviously the girl had other homework to do. Maybe she had a paper route of her own, but at least for a few short paragraphs she wanted something more.

In her account, James woke to the sound of a cat lapping milk outside his bedroom window. She described the sound the cat's tongue made against the surface of the milk: "Lapalapalapalap."

"James had a dream that he was a basketball superstar. He could leap twice as high as any other player. He had to be careful not to crush his head on the hard orange rim. When he got out of bed he felt like he was still sailing through the air, even when his bare feet touched the cold linoleum of his family's kitchen. He smelled cinnamon toast and from a breeze through the screen door he smelled pine needles. He felt fresh and alive, until he saw the expression on his mother's face as his little sister, Cleese, shook the last dust from a box of Lucky Charms."

I never met William. I have no particular reason for doubting that he once charmed a bird out of a tree. Why not? I accelerated off the ramp and onto Highway 101 with the Golden Gate Bridge in sight. The red needle on the temperature gauge remained about a quarter inch above the letter C, but I smelled burning rubber and I saw white steam rising from under the hood. "Baby, Baby, where did our love go?" I don't know, but I felt something corrosive leaking inside of me and I thought that maybe William had charmed a bird once, but that Erik would not have been there to see it. Or if Erik had been there, he would not have seen it.

Where's Fran Haynes?

IT'S TUESDAY, WHICH IS MY SUNDAY, and I'm entering The Shannon Arms to share a liquid lunch with one of my oldest friends, Dorfman. A while back I thought I was on the death slope, the sensation of a blade twisting under the ribs on my lower right side that left as mysteriously as it came, but not without implications, resolutions. I resolved to be the worker of the month at my job. I resolved to catch up with my old friends.

The bar is long and dark with a low ceiling. Dorfman has his bootheels hooked in the rung of his barstool, his head down. He looks like a wet long-haired dog with glasses. He's reading the cover of a matchbook. I want to be eager to see him and I might give him a slap on the shoulder, the big handshake, but the sight of him drains me. I take the matchbook out of his fingers and read an ad for the One Way Truck Driving School—a religious vocational program. He downs the remainder of his stout.

"You're going to drive a truck?" I say.

"Why not?" He's sullen because I'm two beers late. "You're a prick, Kash," he says.

"I'm a prick?"

"You're a prick."

"They won't even let you hold the darts in here anymore," I say. "Am I right?" I ask the bartender. Her face is buried under a pile of hair and she doesn't look up from her newspaper. She circles a word in the WordSearch. I think her name is Rhonda.

"What will it be for you?" she says in a voice like scissors cutting tin. The rumor is that she used to be stunning.

"Give me one of those." I point to Dorfman's glass. "Better make it two."

"Who says I can't hold the darts?" Dorfman lifts his head two inches, drops it.

"I says," says Rhonda, her back to us.

"You want to drive a semi, Dorf?" I say. "Why would you want to do that? You'd lose your disability."

"I have a hearing next week."

"Your ass is still numb, right?"

"Just the left cheek," he says. "I don't want to talk about it."

The bartender puts the first beer down in front of me, but Dorfman scoops it up. He puts a hand on my shoulder. "I'll tell you what," he says.

I wait. How did his nose get so many red lines? He's only thirty years old, same as me. He wipes the foam off his lip with his flannel sleeve.

"I can make you laugh with just two words."

"Marty Dorfman?"

"Harry Chong," he says. He studies my face. Rhonda turns her head from the tap. I think they might have a wager on this.

"This is your idea of funny, Dorfman?" He's so close now, so still, I can see the brain behind the yellow-flecked eyes. He's forgiven me, I think, or he's forgotten.

"Chong Chong," he says.

"What, I'm three years old?" I say. He's fighting a grin, but it's a backed up faucet ready to explode. The fucking idiot. He's the same guy I met at State University ten years ago. We were in the same quad, played on the same flag football team, dated the same woman, though not at the same time. I take my beer from Rhonda and tip it back.

"Chong Chong Chong," he bursts into laughter.

I spit a mouthful of beer back into my glass. The fucking genius.

"That was three words," says Rhonda.

Monday, of course, is my Saturday and Saturday night I spent with Schultz. I left my reading glasses in his apartment and made a plan to meet him this evening at La Valenciana, a white tablecloth establishment. I take the Muni to the bus and then on foot I manage to stay a half step ahead of the rain clouds coming in off the coast. Schultz has a table next to the fireplace, a soft green drink in a round glass on a long thin stem.

"Leo," I say.

"I'm a busy man," he says, looking anything but busy. He licks his thumb and touches his eyebrow—a new tick.

"I'm—"

"How's that sorry ass, Dorfman?" Schultz was also a quad mate, the quarterback of our flag football team. Schultz also dated the woman that Dorfman and I dated, but he dated her first.

"He might be considering a career change," I say.

"From nothing to what?" He beckons the waitress, touches his eyebrow. "Never mind, I'm not really interested," he says. Black skirt, white satin top, she arrives at our table, puts her pen to her pad, shakes her head and I watch as her bangs fall exactly where they had been over her left eye. "I'll have one of those." I point to Schultz's drink.

"How's the ex?" he asks. This is our way of referring to the only woman we ever loved. We don't say her name, presumably out of respect, or because it would be too painful. Sometimes I can't remember her name.

"I told you last night, I don't know," I say.

"All right," he says, "Don't wet yourself."

"How's the teaching business?" I ask.

"I told you all about it last night."

"Tell me again. Now what department are you in?"

"Interdisciplinary Studies."

"Ah, that's right. Now tell me again, what's that all about?"

"Kash, you're pissing me off."

"You started to tell me about a project. A book. You were excited."

"It's nothing," he says.

"A culmination, you said. Hobbes, Hegel, Husserl, Heidegger, Habermas."

"None of the above."

"Hume."

"Nope. I'm looking forward now," he says, embarrassed.

"What's your book called?"

"Forget about it. Forget I ever mentioned it."

"What if somebody wants to know? What if say you-know-who calls me some rainy dark night and asks, 'What's up with our old friend, Schultzy?' What am I going to tell her?"

Schultz shakes his head. "Don't laugh then."

"I won't laugh." He wets his thumb and touches his eyebrow. "Come on already, what's the title of your book?"

"*Making Meaning Mean Something*," he says. He drinks.

"Huh," is all I can say.

"What does that mean?"

"You'll have to excuse me, Leo."

"Nothing is, you know, written in, you know, stone."

I pretend to be wiping my lips with a napkin. I can't stand it. "Do you know what Dorfman said?" I say.

"I think I couldn't care less."

"He said, 'Harry Chong'."

"That's not funny."

"I guess it's not."

"I don't think it's funny at all, Kash."

"No no, I guess you're right. You'll have to excuse me, Leo." I walk to the men's room and lock myself in the stall. I try to think of something that will help me compose myself.

My answering machine greets me with a red number three. After a long pause, I hear Dorfman's crusty "You left your wallet in the bar, you sad sack. Ya wanna know what's funny?" I can barely hear his voice above what sounds like clattering dishes and cackling laughter. "Rhonda thinks your credit is good."

Next is Schultz: "Hey, if you-know-who calls, don't say a word about anything. You're a prick, Kash, you know."

The last message is silence. I get these too often.

It's a wet Wednesday morning, my Monday, and I'm riding the bus to the BART. I'm the Assistant Branch Manager of Canned Foods. I was in the Quality Assurance Department, then I got moved to something called The Concept Team, and now this latest promotion, though my raise hasn't been approved yet. I used to ride in the back of the bus, but when I began to fear I was dying, I started riding up front. I found that talking to the bus driver was a way to avoid unpleasant thoughts. Today there is a new driver.

"Where's Fran Haynes?" I ask her.

"I don't know any Fran Haynes," she says.

"Fran Haynes is the man who usually drives this route."

"I don't know him."

I can't always read people, but I can tell right off that she's not one for chatting. This woman is not going to be my friend. I sit back and watch the windshield wipers. I think about the old days. I think about Dorfman wearing his baggy white shorts on top of his sweat pants, the plastic strap of his mouthguard like a tongue sticking out of his face, his enthusiasm for a muddy flag football game. I can see Schultz wiping his hands on a towel, then zinging a perfect spiral to Dorfman in the flat. Schultz gives me the pitch and I look for the seam. I run behind a pair of dog-mean pulling guards and I wait for Dorfman's crackback block before I make my cut.

We were no ordinary flag football team. We practiced. We had a playbook with fifty plays: straight ahead runs, trap blocks, sweeps, screens, quarterback options, halfback options, reverses and double reverses. We choreographed our steps. We cut classes. We lifted weights. We drank nutritional drinks. We were almost unbeatable.

I can see our ex on the sidelines. She never missed a game. She used to wear the most distracting stockings, candy cane stripes of red and white or purple and orange. She had a floppy coat with a hood big enough for two heads, or one head with a fountain of hair. On the days when the sun blitzed through a hole in the clouds, everyone looked at her hair. She'd holler such things as, "You can do it, Leo," or "You can do it, Marty," or "You're the one, Kash."

The grayness and the whine of the wipers lulls me back. I feel the way I feel immediately after one of the silent phone messages—defenseless. I wonder if I'll feel the stabbing pain in my side.

I feel it.

"It's not what you think, Fran."

"I'm not your friend Fran. I don't know who he is."

"Right." I cramp forward. "Do you mind if I talk to you?"

"I'm not going anywhere," she says.

I try to sit back, but the pain makes me lean forward again. "She used to say she didn't care if we won or lost. Of course we couldn't believe her. How could we? We cared so much. But she said, 'I just love to watch you boys play.' She said, 'I can't explain it, but watching you play makes me so happy.' She didn't have to explain it, though. We could see it. We could feel her happiness."

"To start with, who's she?"

"I made a promise not to say her name. I'm sorry."

"I don't care," she says, but I can see she does. The way she pumps the brakes and sends a man reeling forwards, the way she pulls the lever that closes the door.

"It was 1986. The year I would have graduated from State, had I stuck with it. My friend, Dorfman, blew off his career sciences internship. He dropped out of school. My friend,

Schultz, took a number of incompletes that semester, but the following year he pulled it together and got his degree in…I can't remember what. Schultz always had a little more of what it takes than Dorfman or myself.

"It was December, the week before Christmas break and she was with me then and we were in the championship because we always were, because we practiced. Schultz hated Dorfman when he lost her, but when she left Dorfman for me, Schultz didn't hate Dorfman any less. I'd expected that he'd hate me, but he didn't. Schultz's was a pointed and unequivocal hate. Dorfman hated me and hated himself. He hated Schultz because Schultz hated him. It was a wonder we could play on the same field together, but we hated the idea of losing so we muddled. With grunts and twitches we communicated.

"She wore the red and white candy canes, with Christmas right around the corner…what?…did you say something?"

"Nothing," says the bus driver.

"The team we were facing had a QB who could send it downfield, not pretty—wounded ducks, as they say—but fifty yards in the air. They had a wide receiver named Stickman and it was freaky the way he could jump. But that was all they had. For the first half of the game that little passing connection enabled them to match us score for score. In the second half we figured out how to exploit their weakness—a lineman named Harry Chong.

The driver pulls a lever which causes the bus to kneel down at the curb. She opens the doors. I pause because I think she's not going to take in what I'm saying. "If you want my opinion," she says.

"Yes, I do."

"You boys were a bunch of fools."

"I can't argue with you."

"Didn't you see how she was playing you? Three boyfriends on one team."

"But it wasn't like that. It was, but it wasn't.

"And no doubt she left you right after the game or else you wouldn't be telling this story."

"Are you just filling in for Fran?" I can't be selective. The pain is getting worse and I need to continue.

"Your precious little tart left you for this Harry Chong." A woman and two children step in at the front of the bus. A man in a wheelchair enters the side door. The driver secures the man with straps and buckles, then returns to her seat. "I've known plenty of Harry Chongs," she says. "And plenty little tarts, too."

"No," I say. We've passed my stop, but I need to set the record straight. She puts a stick of gum in her mouth. She chews. I take a deep breath and try to compose myself.

"At halftime the score was twenty-four to twenty-four. She was standing on the sideline with a canvas bag, two long looping handles. She'd brought lunch for all of us, but Schultz and Dorfman wouldn't have any part of it. They milled about, you see. They were so busy milling away from her that they milled into each other. I saw them talking for the first time in months. She and I decided to have our picnic under one of the goalposts. A lovely repast of potato salad with crushed coriander and some sliced cucumber. We talked about the holiday break, how I might catch a Greyhound to Grass Valley and share a glass of eggnog with her mom and dad at midnight on Christmas Eve. Neither Schultz nor Dorfman ever met her family."

"And I'm guessing that you never met them either." The driver leans into a wide turn. She sits back in her seat. "In fact, I'm sure of it."

"Well," I say, "you're right, but," I can't help adding, "Fran Haynes is a good listener. He's not so concerned about being right."

"And I'll tell you what else. This Harry Chong no doubt steals your candy cane."

"There you're wrong."

"Am I?"

I lean forward and lean back and lean forward again. I'm watching the way she chews. I want to see her bite her tongue. "Harry Chong never played, probably never even watched a game of football in his life before that day. Their team had lost one of its linemen in what has come to be known as The Groin Pull Incident—another story. Harry Chong was a quad mate. A body. He was big, well over two hundred and fifty pounds. He had the face of a man who can't laugh. He was shirtless, rolls of fat over the waistband of his yellow shorts. He couldn't or wouldn't get into a proper three point stance; instead, he squatted, his butt inches above his muddy sneakers. He was unbalanced."

She slows the bus, but her gum chewing continues full speed ahead. "Do you think all of this is relevant?"

"Crucial," I say. "You see, it's only because we could effortlessly knock Harry Chong flat on his back that we won and that we lost."

"All I can see is foolish boys."

"It was Schultz that said that all we had to do was blitz on Harry Chong and we could be kissing the quarterback before he took a step back from center. Perhaps this was the subject of his halftime conference with Dorfman, I don't know. Dorfman suggested the two man blitz. We didn't need to blitz two. Any one of us could and did singly send Harry reeling backward into the slop. I can see him now, waddling to his team's huddle, mud smeared on his back and caking in his hair. I can see him squatting, blank-faced, ready to be flattened again."

"And your part?" Fran Haynes had never asked me what was my part. At the worst he would wag his head in a kind of bored bewilderment.

"I invented the code," I say. "There was no secret to it, though we did whisper at first. By the end of the game we were shouting it. 'Chong' meant blitz on Harry Chong. And 'Chong Chong' meant two men blitz on Harry Chong. And 'Chong

Chong Chong'…you get the picture."

"I suppose I do."

"We humiliated him. We won the game. We lost her. I lost her. We lost playing. Let me out at the next stop." I'm holding my ribs as I step down into the stairwell, my back to the driver.

"Do you want my opinion?" she says.

"No."

"Foolish boys."

The decision to promote me to Assistant Branch Manager, I was told, was based upon two facts; I never miss work and I am never late. It was also noted that I made exceptional contributions to The Concept Team. I am ten blocks from work at the corner of Mission and South Van Ness wiping rain out of my hair.

It was I who suggested that the generic food items be shelved on one aisle called "Basics." Shoppers who buy no-name brands know exactly where to find what they are looking for. They save an average of fifteen minutes per week. It was my idea to display toothpaste and toothbrushes beside the assorted candies in the checkout lines. These items have more than doubled their inventory. I pored over the schedules until I found a way that two workers could share the same break time. Morale, of course, is immeasurable, but it has noticeably improved. I was worker of the month last month, my three-by-five photo is mounted in the center of a white slip of posterboard above the Noodles-In-A-Cup display.

It is Wednesday, which is my Monday. Two buses and a Muni later, I'm not surprised to find Dorfman slouched over his favorite stool in The Shannon Arms. I am surprised to see Schultz seated next to him.

"Yurly," Dorfman says. And then to Schultz, "Zurly." He looks back in my direction and says something that sounds like, "You look awful."

"I thought you were going to ask for a raise today," says Schultz. "Looks kind of like you blew it."

"What about your book, Leo," I say. "Why don't we talk about that?"

"Never mind."

"You're a busy man," I force a laugh.

"It's all over," Leo says. "Kaput." I expect him to lick his finger and touch his eyebrow, but he doesn't.

"I guess I have to agree with you," I say. "It's over."

Dorfman belches. "Suckers," he says, almost loud enough to get Rhonda's attention. He sits up too straight too fast. Schultz and I catch him before he falls on his back. I'm reminded of the time Dorfman first injured himself on a kick-off return. Schultz and I carried him off the field. I think we loved each other then.

"Harry Chong," Dorfman says.

"It's not funny anymore," I say.

"It never was," says Schultz.

We watch Rhonda cut a lime in halves, quarters, eighths.

"How 'bout a game a darts?" Dorfman says.

Rhonda shakes her head.

"Come on, Sweetie," Dorfman says. He looks at Schultz. He looks at me.

"I think it will be OK," Schultz says to Rhonda. "We're the only ones in here."

Rhonda looks long and hard at each one of us. "I don't think it's a good idea," she says.

"It's a good idea," I assure her. "Yes, it will all be fine. Watch us play."

The Amateur Ventriloquist

TEN YEARS AGO ON A SATURDAY NIGHT CYNTHIA and I got a babysitter for Bubble and went out for a good time. The trouble was, we couldn't agree on what constituted a good time. I know I drank most of a pint of Old Crow and I put down some beer. I wanted time off, time out. I wanted to go back to a time when life was simple and romance was romantic. Cynthia wasn't drinking. She had said she wanted time for us to be alone together, something about getting reacquainted. She said I was not the man she married and she was not the woman I married. And I said, Come on Cindy, come on, you're just as beautiful as ever.

We tried to go to an old pine roadhouse we had frequented when we were first dating—red felt pool tables, an electric fireplace, a dilapidated shack really, but we thought it had charm. We couldn't find it. We parked down off Old River Road in a dusty lot beneath the unfinished bridge. I remember that we screamed at each other and in the morning my throat was sore. In the morning Cynthia put on a sleeveless yellow shift and a smile. "Let's go to the country fair," she said. "Let's do something different for a change."

I said, "Come on, I've had enough of the snakes," and I picked up reluctant Bubble and left the Deadly Snake Pavilion. Cynthia waited under the edge of the canopy until the last inch of python slithered into its basket. The August sun was stinging my scalp. Bubble and I watched a horse drop a steaming pile.

"Look, Daddy."

"Let's go to the Petting Zoo," Cynthia said. She put her hand on my elbow and with a skip in her step led us into the human thoroughfare. The line was one hundred feet long and the end of it happened to be very near to the end of the line for cold drinks.

"You guys wait on this line and I'll get us a couple of sno-cones," I said. "I'll meet you down there." I had seen a man leave the silver trailer with a tall golden beer in a plastic cup, and though only hours before I had sworn to Cynthia that I would quit, we hadn't agreed on any specifics, like when.

A dozen and a half school children and their attendant quickly filled the space between my family and me. Within moments I couldn't see the lavender ribbon Cynthia wore in her hair. I saw a husky teen carry an empty beer keg from the back of the silver trailer. My line began to move quickly. There's nothing wrong with a country fair if you get in the right frame of mind, I thought. Cotton candy and cow pies, young lovers with hands in each other's back pockets, it's all so lovely, so life-affirming.

I managed the two sno-cones in my left hand, a sugary pink running down my forearm. I put the beer down quickly; cold, numbing, delicious, and set the cup atop an overstuffed metal barrel, corn cobs and flies. Lavender ribbon—I scanned the line at eye level. Then I scanned again, lower, looking for Bubble's big pink barrette. There were the school children—a skirmish over a plastic sword. There was the attendant pressing her fingertips against the base of her skull, but I couldn't find my wife and daughter. Bubble probably had a diaper event, I thought. Probably Cynthia took her to the comfort station. Through the chicken wire and red, white and blue bunting that framed the petting zoo, I spied a toddler touching the knee of an ostrich, a father and his daughter stroking the chin of a pot-bellied piglet. Cynthia must be searching for me. I made my way, slowly at first, back toward the cold drinks trailer. Let me get some napkins for these sno-cones, another beer while I'm at it.

I walked back toward the petting zoo, and this time a little beyond. I was getting farther from the rattle of the rollercoaster and the shrieks from the Sea Dragon, almost enjoying myself. A shoeless young couple, she tugging his big belt buckle, a swarm of couples, a convention of sorts formed in the center of the path, dozens of bare feet. Flicking of bangs, flicking of ashes, whispers, laughter, scandal: young love could be so intoxicating. I stopped at another silver trailer.

On my right a small crowd dispersed, a juggler put double-bladed hatchets and torches into his customized briefcase. I began walking more quickly, more anxious to find my family. A woman with a purple turban and a cotton sari beckoned me, long, pointed black nails. Most of them tell you what they think you want to hear. The others are terrifying. I saw the lavender ribbon through the planks and poles of a small set of bleachers.

Cynthia was center stage sitting on a bale of hay, freckles of sunlight on her pale, slender arms. She was as beautiful as the day we met. Bubble sat on her lap. A man with a red bandana held out a microphone and Cynthia tried to speak but burst out laughing. "Try it again," said the man. "It comes from down in here." He made a round sweep with his hand that encompassed his throat and chest. His voice had a slightly higher pitch than one might have expected. His mouth did not move when he spoke.

"I don't know what to say," Cynthia said, and again convulsed in laughter.

"That was very good," said the man. "Let's give Cynthia some encouragement," he said to the twenty-five to thirty seated on the planks. The crowd clapped. "Just say whatever is on your mind."

Cynthia straightened her back and peered out into the strange faces. Her eyes found me, but she made no sign of recognition. She was bracing herself for her performance. Without any movement of the lips and only the slightest flexure of her larynx, she said loudly and clearly, "There's my husband, standing over there." Bubble looked perplexed, a little frightened when the crowd applauded. The crowd turned their eyes on me and I looked down at the liquid sno-cones in my hands. Then I breathed deeply, a swell of emotion. There's my wife, my lovely daughter, radiant. I've missed them.

"Do a real trick, Mommy," Bubble said. The crowd laughed, but Cynthia did not.

"You're very good at this," said the man on stage. "Now is there anything you'd like to say to your husband?" He pushed the mike back in front of Cynthia, but held it low so that we could all watch her mouth. I watched her eyes.

At age thirteen, Bubble prefers to be called Katy. She left her mother's house in California, got a friendly man to buy her a ticket on the Trailways, and appeared in my doorway, room 729, Riverside Hospital, NYC. I am trying to adjust the picture on the television when I see her. She is tall like her mother. She has pale, slender arms. Her hair is the color mine was, like straw.

Katy does a real trick. Her speech is shimmering tears. Then she walks.

"No," I say. "No," I holler. "Not again." And though I can't remember where my apartment is, or what I wanted out of life, there are things I can't forget: that the back of my gown is open and shows my bare ass; the ache I felt when I found them in the spotted sunlight; and what Cynthia said, the last time she threw her voice: "You had a chance to know me," she said. "He did."

What to Say When You Talk to Yourself

DEAR JOSH,

It's Tuesday night, April 1st, mild weather even by northern Cal standards. Thank you for the recent—not so recent because I'm slow in responding—letter and pictures. Once upon a time I didn't think Jason looked very much like you, and now I think he does. He looks exactly as you did, but perhaps a few years younger and few pounds heavier than you when you were riding your bicycle in uniform in France, or was it Belgium, scouting a little peace in the war. Do you remember when you told me that story? And there's Peg with her hand on Jason's shoulder, her chin thrust forward, her eyes bright even in the afternoon sun—her listening face. You guys are what I think of when I think of family. Do you ever find yourself on the other side of the camera? I'd like very much to have a picture of you, though as you can see, I'm a shameless prevaricator and won't hesitate to develop my own. But it's not for me that I'm asking. It's often enough I tell stories that include my "good friend back in New York" that my classmates, David, or my sisters or Linda will say, "Oh, do you mean the counselor?" It'd be nice for me to be able to share a picture with your name. It'd be nice for me to have, too.

You opened your last letter saying you were worried about me. I'm often very happy, but as I think you know, I'm easily overwhelmed and I find it hard to focus. I suspect you meant you were worried about my drinking. I can assure you that with Linda and the baby, that's very much under control.

April 17th. I started this letter two and half weeks ago, and only now find time to continue. Linda and Lucy are with Linda's parents in Kansasville, Wisconsin. They'll be back a week from Monday, not soon enough. I guess I'm getting along with the cats. Spoke with Linda's mother on the phone today—Linda happened to be strolling Lucy around the cornfield—and she told me that Lucy's first words when she got off the plane were, "Daddy home?" No, I want to tell her. You took home with you.

The upside is that I've had plenty of time to write. The down: I'm producing a lot of crap. Why does that happen? I have a million starts, but nothing that takes root. People are full of shit, Josh. I know you don't like it when I say things like that. *Most people* are full of shit. You were the only one who didn't give me an unequivocal thumbs up when I said I wanted to be a writer. I've tried, as you suggested, remembering my dreams, but these days I have no access to that world. Usually I start writing a conversation that's in my head, wait and see where it leads. I might as well be talking to you.

I was walking today, kicking stones in a culvert when I saw a station wagon that was standard shift. You don't see that so often, and it took me back because I used to drive such a car, custard-yellow, back in '88 while working for an outfit called C-L-E-C; The Citizens' & Labor Energy Coalition, in NYC. Magically, I'm back in that car driving on the Long Island Expressway with a cargo of names and faces I'd filed and forgotten: Jules, our tow-headed, smooth-talking captain who could deftly compare the deregulation of natural gas prices to the dereg of airline fares, facts and figures spilling from his perfect dentition; Maryanne, the woman with a laugh like a jackhammer; Geoff, I can only remember his bottle-thick glasses and a garlic smell; Chris, the self-described queer, every day with a new ribald adventure from Hell's Kitchen to report, he used to dig his steel-toed Timberlands under my seat; Toby, shy kid from Scranton, PA., didn't last long; Tami, pigtails and pimply, she had a terrible crush on Jules; and

Lillia, coming slowly back into focus, apple-scented shampoo and a bruise-colored aura.

I can recall that time like it's happening now. The sun rose clean and bright and cut new shadows all around me. I was but wasn't my sisters' little brother, Will and Bea's devoted son, my teachers' student, my bosses' worker, etc. We were driving from NYC to the boroughs to canvass, to stop the deregulation of natural gas prices, to solicit the trust and the cash of people who were foolish enough to answer their doors. It wasn't new for me to feel like a stranger in the world. I was by then a professional hitch-hiker, the transient soul you met, "candid, but dissonant," you'd said, but it was new and odd for me to introduce myself seventy to eighty times per night, five nights a week for ten months. Hello, my name is Bill, I'm with C-L-E-C. I'm here to interrupt your dinner, your dessert, your bathing of baby, your television requiem. I'm here to win you over, stranger in a strange world.

You and Peg must get such visitors occasionally. Maybe Jason is out rapping on doors right now. NYPIRG? Greenpeace? The canvassers need to raise quota in order to keep their jobs. They may or may not feel urgency about the cause they represent, but if they are going to have any success, they'd better get a little turned on by their power to persuade and seduce. As for me, I wasn't moved by the regulations concerning natural gas prices. I wasn't a home owner—my rat-hole in Harlem. It was all an abstraction. I remember that I told people that my name is Bill, then I deluged them with facts: the price of gas at the wellhead; the cost of deep sand drilling; the projected profits for Shell and Exxon if prices became deregulated, etc., and many of those people rewarded me with a check or a five spot. For my part, they might have said: You're right, your name is Bill, let me give you some money.

Is that my story? He's Bob, not Bill. Bob fell for Lillia. Lillia Montero-Sanchez. I don't think I ever mentioned her name, but

I was always talking about her. She was not the first "L" of my life, not the first consuming crush I'd ever had. There had been a Ms. Lydia in the second grade and before her an Aunt Lynn, but Lillia was probably the first and certainly my last twenty-four/seven obsession. She was an ex-heroin addict (or would you say there are no ex-addicts?), a singer and acoustic guitarist, an old soul in the figure of a twenty-nine-year-old woman. She lived on the lower east side in one of those apartments that has a toilet in the kitchen. *Bob only saw her apartment once.* She had straight auburn hair she tossed with the back of her hand. The shock of her eyes—*I'm still working on her eyes.* She was born in Cuba and raised there until age six when her mother brought her to South Carolina. She had a Cuban accent and spoke very quickly, but her sentences ended like socks on a polished wood floor, that slow, Southern drawl.

Bob worked mornings as a volunteer "recreation specialist" at Bellevue Hospital during this time of discovery. Daily from ten to noon he'd make the rounds on the eleventh and twelfth floors hearing stories, sharing smiles and cigarettes. It was one of the ways he'd hoped to run into himself, or that's how he would have explained if anyone had asked, because Bob believed that beneath all his selves was a core self, an unselfish self, a complete and unto-itself self which would emerge unfettered under the right circumstances—a self he might see walking purposefully down a long white corridor. Sometimes he'd see his image in a white jacket with his name tag pinned to the breast pocket reflected in the stainless steel elevator doors. There's me, he'd think, not asking, giving, not needing, needed; but in fact Bob's role at Bellevue was not well defined.

His supervisor, Virginia, spent most of her time chatting with nurses over coffee in the rec. office. Bob was never trained, merely taken around and introduced. Recreation Specialist: what in the hell did that mean? There were a few bedrooms where Bob would knock lightly and enter with confidence, but many others where he paused and rocked from foot to foot wondering who he was and what he had to offer. He'd put in his two hours, then stop for lunch, or a drink at the Holiday Cocktail Lounge, transmission fluid he called it, before heading to his job uptown at the C-L-E-C office.

One day as Jules was distributing flyers to the canvassers, some important new facts about how the big oil companies had suppressed info regarding alternative energy sources, Bob popped it to Lillia: Would she be willing to play and sing at Bellevue? She loved the idea. Bob had to whisper and Lillia moved close, put her hand on his, her apple-scented shampoo.

The following day Bob hopped and skipped his rounds on eleven and twelve. He even entered the room of the woman with cancer at the top of her spine, that awful head brace with bolts drilled into her skull. She never blinked. Hello, my name is Bob, he said, and in this place where people so often made up their minds to stop living, he was a spring morning, birds, buds on trees and sunshine. Hello, my name is Bob and my friend, Lillia is coming...Hello, my friend, Lillia...he repeated thirty-six times per floor, seventy-two times per day for three days.

Bob greeted Lillia at the elevator, took the guitar case from her hand and then gave it back, realizing that he'd need both hands in his ecstatic rush to pull IV racks and push wheelchairs to the lounge on the corner of twelve overlooking the East River. He wasn't anybody's anybody, purely Bob, when Lillia strummed and Jim Spivey, the old black man with hepatitis and feet like an elephant, tapped his skinny knees and watched Lillia's fingers work. Lillia was so damn smart. Everyone in the room wanted the light from her eggplant-colored eyes (yuk, Josh, can I get away with that description?). Her eyes were so brown they were black, so black they were purple. What a disservice our language does to that lovely vegetable because you take cans and soft plastic bags of bread and cold cylindrical things from your grocery basket back there in the Queens Safeway or D'Agostino's or whatever, but you can't wait to hold the eggplant. That was Lillia. Supple and shining. Perfect as a tear on a baby's cheek, that smart, when she looked up from her guitar at the woman Bob wheeled down the long corridor from Suicide Watch, cop trailing, handcuffs clinking in cop fingers. I didn't think I'd ever get that woman down the hall because the last time she'd gotten out of bed she was on a one-way trip to the subway tracks, but it was a magical time and she was in a trance and I said, Hello, my name is…Hello, my name is Lillia and the name of my song is "Tomorrow."

Bob loved Lillia, in a manner of speaking. Lillia had loved her father who left her. She had loved drugs and now she was going steady with recovery, a sense of clarity and purpose, some days. She was an avid reader of self-help books and at the time she was enjoying one called *What To Say When You Talk To Yourself*. At Bellevue Bob tried to guess what her inner voice was saying. Her eyes seemed to whisper, "I want to touch you," but the conversation didn't stop there, other voices, older voices demurred. She understood the simple syllogism: Desire implies vulnerability; vulnerability implies relapse. Therefore misery.

Mine is the familiar story of unrequited love. Bob pitched his best raps at Lillia and in words she retreated, but what about her eyes? Lillia's shimmering eyes had seen Bob at his most self-assured and what would he do now, stand in the doorway and rock from foot to foot? Bob got his hands on some cocaine, a guy that visited the landlord, sometimes lived in the basement, a black kid who blasted Pink Floyd (do you know them, Josh, a trippy British band long after your time). Bob wondered if Lillia really loved women because this had been his experience of women in NYC, but Lillia had once told Bob that Jules was "so cute," for such a "white bread chump."

Love made Bob nervous. Nervousness made him lose his appetite. He looked hungry. The bones beneath his cheeks emerged like bare knees under a thin sheet. At twenty-two, two hundred miles from his nearest family, three semesters since he'd dropped college, he was handsomer than he'd ever been in his life. His eyes were green with flecks of brown like the part of the Chesapeake where he grew up.

It was freezing rain, a week after New Year's when Bob knocked on Lillia's door with most of a month's rent, an eightball in his pocket. He waited and waited on that dark little Eldridge Street, sniffed, wandered like a goddamn spaniel. Did he know the rhythm that drove him to The Knitting Factory and back to Eldridge and back to the bar and back again to peer through the thin curtain and the criss-cross metal grate of her window was the rhythm of her song, "Rollercoaster"?

OK, Josh, why is Bill revisiting this time? Climbing again to the top of the Brooklyn Bridge? The Krylon on the stones said, "You climbed this far, now see if you can fly." The cops. The cuffs. That psychiatrist with stripes under his eyes the color of prunes and those stupid-ass questions. Do you ever get depressed? Do you ever feel like your TV is talking to you? Fuck it. *Nothing takes you higher than a rollercoaster ride/ Don't know you've reached the top till you're going down the other side.*

Of course it wasn't long after my release that I met you. Linda will be home soon. Did I tell you that Lucy is in the ninety-fifth percentile for her height and weight, twenty-nine pounds. She's got the hugest cheeks. You've seen the pictures. She's learned to kiss, but there's no pucker, just a soft, wet skid. Don't worry about me, Josh.

Let's say that Bob snorts his entire eightball. This is fiction, right? I don't remember how much is in an eightball, a lot. He's flying, not at first, but over time, flying through the subway tunnels from his rat-hole in Harlem to Eldridge Street, black puddles fill the broken black asphalt, neon at the far end, he's shivering. There's not enough light and no color so that every time a figure Bob's height, take an inch, with long straight hair, but she could have gotten it cut, she could be in there. He knocks on her window and paces some more. Motivation? Bob is desperate. This is not really a love story. Lillia is Bob's invention. This is a coming of age tale. Bob realizing Bob, but....

Bob had been faltering with C-L-E-C. Four nights passed and he hadn't made his eighty-two-dollar quota. The crew had been in what Jules called "working class turf" where pitches had to be hard and contributions were always small. Toby had already been dropped from the crew and Bob would be next, but no one wanted to see him lose his job. He was young and quiet, maybe a little uptight, an odd sense of humor sometimes, but he was part of the team. Hello, my name is Bob, I'm with...Jules was the first to retrain him. He stressed basics. "Get the clipboard in their hands. Hold the pen. Watch me." Bob watched Jules slide one check after another under the clasp of his clipboard. "Once you get on a roll, they come easily," Jules said.

"Find a theme and milk it," said Chris. "I use *neighbors* because I loved Mr. Rogers." Bob tagged along with Chris for five doors until the words echoed in his head: "I'm in the *neighborhood*. Your *neighbors* have been chipping in. The oil companies are raking it in, while you and your *neighbors*." Chris surprised Bob when he said: "It's not a conceptual thing, it's a confidence thing. No one's going to give you a damn penny if you don't believe you deserve it."

Bob retrained for part of an hour with Maryanne. What her trick was he couldn't say, but it seemed to be her jackhammer laugh. "Hi Bob, you're with who?" said a fat man through his glass door. The man bit into a sandwich and a piece of tomato fell onto his white shirt. Bob laughed the laugh he'd heard from Maryanne and the wooden door closed in his face.

Lillia had taken a few days off, to nurse a cold, she said. She hadn't been answering her telephone. When she returned to work she looked pale, slightly ocherous like the weather-beaten hood of the station wagon. The crew was rolling toward the night's turf in Rego Park, Bob ironically at the helm, Jules riding shotgun, Lillia squeezed between the others in the backseat, her clipboard on her knees. "Train with Lillia tonight," Jules had said to Bob. Bob found her dark eyes in the rearview, a weak smile.

They stood at the corner, intersection of one-hundred-thirty-second and fifty-fourth. "Good luck," said Maryanne, Tami, and Geoff. Chris winked. Jules saluted. When the others had paced off to their first doorsteps, deep breaths, clipboards held high, Lillia took Bob's hand in hers. "You're shaking," she said. "Do what I do." She closed her eyes and breathed in, and again...*and if she was breathing like that then she must be really real just like...and she must have feelings like....* "Close your eyes," she said when she saw he was staring at her. "Try this: Nam Myo Renge Kyo," she said. "It's a chant I learned from a Krishna on the subway. Say it." She put her hand flat on his back. "Say it." He said it. "Don't whine," she said. "No whining. Peace."

They canvassed four houses together. "My name is Lillia and this is Bob and we're out to stop big ull from stealing more of your money. The only way we can beat big ull is if we all come together." She got a check for ten from a woman whose children were fighting for controls of a video game in the background and she got three dollars and fifty cents from an old man whose head was still shaking from the injustice of it all as Lillia and Bob reached the end of his sidewalk.

"I called you," Bob said.

"I haven't been feeling well." She started toward the other side of the street. "I'll work this side."

He nodded, took a deep breath.

"Maybe you could call me again," she said, "you know, in a while." That night he DQ'ed—doubled the quota. In the interstices of his urgent rap he could hear her words, "we" and "come together." And it might have lasted, but of course it didn't.

Josh, I can hear you. I'm stalling, right? I can see you looking at the clock above the etching of the clown on the wall of your office. Bob asked Jules if he could train with Lillia again, but Jules said that Lillia didn't feel comfortable with him. And when Bob pressed her she said, "Lillia needs to take care of Lillia right now"—the way that Liilia speaks when she talks to herself. Afterward, she avoided him at work as much as possible. She screened her phone calls, sometimes drunken, desperate calls. Quota became too much for Bob. The long, white corridors at Bellevue, too long. And in the rain, between the dim puddles at the far end of Eldridge Street with a song in his head, Bob heard Lillia's wooden heels approaching.

"Lillia?"

"Who's that?"

"You didn't return my calls. I was worried about you."

"No, Bob." She walked down three steps and unlocked the deadbolt, then put another key in the knob. He stood on the top step behind her. "You shouldn't have come," she said.

"I had some blow, but I guess I—"

"No, you shouldn't have."

"Are you going to invite me in?"

"No." She stepped inside and spoke through the crack. "I'm tired. I'm sorry."

"Just to warm up for a minute." He rubbed his hands together.

"I'm sorry."

"My name is Bob, I'm with—"

"No, no, my baby is in the bath and I'm on a long distance phone call and, come on, Bob, it's not what I want."

"Let me in, Lillia, cause there's nowhere."

"Stop it, stop, STOP IT!"

And he pushed through the door, confident from the coke, maybe—it's been so long since I've had any—and from the shots of Tanqueray at the bar, and bleary, but not unfocused, determined to win her over. "Just do the Krishna chant," he said to her. She backed away into her bedroom, closed the door and picked up the telephone. He followed, but turned a slow three-sixty because he'd spent many late hours imagining this place. Bookshelves made from rough-cut sheets of plywood and stolen milk crates. A handmade mobile with the cardboard heads of rock stars cut from favorite album covers. A kimono on the back of a wooden chair. A coffee cup and half a cabbage on the draining board. A pouch of tobacco and some papers on a table. Rhinestone boots beneath the table, folded in upon themselves as if exhausted. There was the toilet only three feet from the kitchen sink. The Tracy Chapman poster she'd once described to him, toughness and innocence.

"My name is Bob," he knocked on her bedroom door, "and I'm not with anyone." This seemed the perfect time to inject the Maryanne jackhammer laugh he'd been practicing. As he came through the door, Lillia set the receiver back in its cradle.

"Come on, then," she said. She lifted her feet off the floor and parted her legs on the futon. She stretched her hands way up above her head and feigned a yawn, then a sleepy seductive smile. "I'm ready now," she said. Bob was ready too, and willing to believe because the lesson that he'd learned over and over was *believing makes it real*, but he heard a clamoring from the floor above, an elephant tumbling down the stairs. He might have savored this picture of Lillia, the supine stretch and smile, the shimmer of her eyes, it was only exactly as he'd dreamed it, but he didn't have time to soak it in after all. He turned at the sound of the front door flying against the plaster wall, the sight of that man in plaid boxers and a sleeveless T and of all things, on the lower east side of New York, a golf club, slicing the air as it came closer.

Bob was hit once. He walked out on his own two feet, one hand riding the wall and the other pressed to his cheek. This would be the biggest shiner of his life. He showed very poor judgment, you're thinking. Yes, that's putting it mildly, but one thing can be said for Bob. He learned. He never went back there.

Not even in his dreams.

Josh, I'm not feeling well. Monday is more than a week and Linda and Lucy are two thousand miles away. Send pictures. Call. It's been good talking to you this way, but it'd be better to hear your voice.

Your friend,
Bill

The Smilies Meet the Brooders

CAB SMILIE LEAVES HIS HOME, GLIDES TO THE DOOR of Joseph and Katja Brooder for a cup of, let's say, sugar.

Barbara Smilie's running water in the bathroom. Or cleaning her oven. Or pushing the vacuum. No, she's sitting on the bed, staring at a laurel leaf pressed against the window pane, but something interferes with her hearing and her vision, like a buzzing blurring in the periphery. She doesn't know she's unhappy until the telephone rings.

It is a vibrant, chilling first Saturday of November, nine-thirty A.M. Joseph Brooder prepares to split wood. He doesn't see Cab pass the open mouth of his garage. He trains his eye to find the upright handle of the maul and the splintered steel blade of the wedge. Sometimes this eye-training thing works. He can find what he wants if he can see it in his mind. He can spare himself the trouble of upsetting piles of stuff he doesn't want, boxes Katja has collected over the years, which have never been properly stored. He feels suddenly alone in the dark and at such times, sometimes, he thinks, What a clever man I am. At other times, like this morning, he thinks, Why do my tools hide from me?

It hasn't yet occurred to Cab that he woke up high from last night's drinking. He's never in his life borrowed a cup of anything from anyone and now the thought that carries him in his faux-fur-lined vinyl slippers, down the new jet black asphalt, past the open garage of his neighbors, beneath the arbor of tangled vines and up to the front door with the hand-carved wooden placard, *THE BROODERS*, is: Why not? Many thoughts bark in his mind, exciting little thoughts like: Life is too short not to feel free to borrow a cup of say, sugar, from a neighbor, and, Look, this is the house they inhabit just as we inhabit ours, and, What if there were no walls? One thought in particular troubles and excites Cab. He had seen a dark figure in the garage which he correctly assumed to be the back of Joseph Brooder. He might have said, "Good morning, Mr. Brooder," or, "Howdy neighbor," because he was feeling unusually light in the step, but as his knuckles prepare to kiss the door, he is keenly aware that he wants to borrow a cup of something from Katja. He has studied her since the day he and Barbara moved in. She is sad eyes and black hair wrapped up in a silk kerchief. She is grace, beauty and shivering feminine sexuality. She is from elsewhere.

Katja Brooder sits in her kitchen about to write a list, half in dreamland. Coffee, pen, paper. Her lap is empty of cats and books. She is unaware that Joseph stepped out of the house into the garage. She anticipates his deep, quiet voice. She plans a trip to the market and deliberates asking what he wants. What he wants is probably what he wanted when he touched her thigh in bed, but she could imagine it all from start to finish, so much effort and concentration for that quick little surge, she couldn't imagine enjoying it. A new kind of cheese, she thinks, gar bags, cat f, red w. The knock at the door—she expects Joseph to answer it. She listens. There's a soft slat in the hardwood floor, water-logged tongue or groove that winces when Joseph steps on it. No wince. As she moves toward the door, she thinks, Who could it possibly be?

*   *   *

The Smilies are new in the neighborhood. Their garage is filled with crates and boxes, one of which houses their own hand-carved wooden placard, *THE SMILIES*. Cab had wanted to unpack it first, to recite something silly in Barbara's ear and pour a libation, before placing it over the door of their new home. He had promised to carry Barabara across the threshold, over the lovely Mexican tiles of the foyer and kitchenette, over the new plush double-foam-backed wall-to-wall, all the way to the king-size bed. Barbara'd giggled at the idea of Cab carrying her. She'd never been carried by a man other than her father, and that was many years ago. And Cab'd experienced a rush, like an extra pulse in his heart as the pictures played through his mind, but then, somehow, he'd forgotten.

The day of moving in, he'd been given the afternoon off from his job as buyer at Drexel Home Furnishings. He and Barb had already loaded the U-Haul, but he'd felt he needed more time, deserved more time. An afternoon isn't enough time to move, but it's adequate to begin celebrating. He'd stopped at the 4th Street Saloon for one martini, dry and dirty. Then another because the bartender was young with an earring in her nose, and to Cab's surprise, she was friendly. He didn't often chat with people of her generation, and certainly none so attractive. She had recently helped a friend move, and yea, it's more exhausting than people think. "It's bullshit," she said. "And they only gave you the afternoon. That's total bullshit." When Cab described his work, she said she'd been searching for a convertible sofa-sleeper. And Cab had said, "You mean a sleeper-sofa." And they laughed when she said she'd already had a sofa-sleeper, her boyfriend, until she kicked him out. Cab and the bartender exchanged numbers on matchbooks, ostensibly to consult on home furnishing bargains. She rapped on the bar signaling that the next round would be on her. After three drinks, Cab felt cozy, except for the vague sense that someone was waiting for him. He also felt, To hell with it, one afternoon and they expect you to move your whole goddamn life into a new house. He had one more. He rapped on the bar and said, "Do. Call me. I'm serious."

When he arrived at the old homestead, there was still a stripe of pale blue in the far corner of the sky. He said, "Thank god," when he saw a light on inside. He'd feared he'd find Barbara sitting on the passenger side of the U-Haul, legs crossed, tapping her knee. He parked. Inside the house was swept and dusted, empty, as if no one had ever lived there. Barbara sat, her large frame curled up tight on the kitchen linoleum. With her wrist she brushed her forehead to push back her bangs, but she'd cut off her bangs a week ago, part of preparation for her new life in a new house in a new town. She looked up at Cab with thick, shining eyes.

"I'm so sorry I'm late." He was urgent.

"You're late?" she sniffed.

"Well," he made his eyes focus hard, then they softened. His face softened. "I'd hoped to get out early." He knelt down beside her and squeezed the taut muscles of her shoulders and the back of her neck. "One thing is always leading to another."

The tears in her eyes rolled down her face. "This is going to sound silly," she said, "but now that the house is empty and clean, I'm reminded of the day I moved in. I was so excited to be in California. I dreamed I'd be happy here. I thought this was going to be home."

"Yea," said Cab. "Well, California is a big place." Then, after a deep breath and a sigh, "You sure knocked yourself out. Look at this house."

"And I remember the day you moved in. We had such high hopes, didn't we?"

"I have high hopes," he said.

"I know you do. I count on you for that, Cab."

"I hope you saved some strength for the new place."

"I didn't love it here," Barbara said, "but I tried. I guess even that makes it hard to let go."

Cab stroked her back and shoulders, kissed her on the ear with his gin breath. "You're not letting go," he said, he smiled his winningest smile. "You're holding on." He helped her to her feet and gave her his elbow as they made their last walk to the door. "You're holding on to me."

Joseph Brooder is an unlikely man to have such a beautiful and gracious wife. He's not unpleasant looking himself, he is very well-kept, but he is not what one would call attractive. Since his days as a mechanic in the air force, he has worn his sand-colored hair very short. His flannel shirts always look freshly cleaned and pressed. This year he will turn fifty and though he's fit, he looks every day his age. Pinches of flesh droop from his overdeveloped jaw muscles. His eyes sit deep in the ravines of his face, small and colorless. He drives a beige pickup owned by the gas and electric. He mumbles. He looks like a man with a secret, and if there is any evidence of such, it would be on the rare occasions when he laughs, loud and shrill.

Barbara said, "Joseph Brooder is a good neighbor." Cab couldn't disagree. She said, "He looks like so many men I knew growing up in the midwest. Good, hardworking men. Democrats even, some of them. He's not unlike my dad."

"But this is California," Cab said. "And that was thirty years ago." He shrugged. Then he said, "They seem like an unlikely couple."

"Why?"

"I'm just saying that she's like Hollywood beautiful, like breathtaking, but he's sure nothing to write home about."

"He's a good man."

"I suppose each of us sees what she wants to believe." Cab grinned.

"I know a good man when I see one."

Cab hugs Barbara from behind, gently grinds his pelvis into her backside. "I won't argue with that," he said.

Barbara and Cab lived in the east county and moved to the

west county, a much shorter drive to Cab's work. They lived in a slow, quiet farming community near a small town with a Five and Dime, a pair of saloons, a gas station and video rental, a twenty-four-hour diner, and a hair cutters. Barbara cut hair. Most of her customers were men, many of whom looked similar to Joseph Brooder, though their flannel shirts were often ripped or soiled and smelled like hay. They tended to sit quietly in the chair and rarely gave an indication if they were pleased or displeased with their haircuts. They were polite. They were gentlemen, yet Barbara often had the odd sensation when she placed her hand flat on the top of a man's head, gave a little twist to the right or the left, that she was stewarding a willful animal. Her first true love had been a horse named Nifty; proud and unpredictable.

Since the move, Barbara cuts the hair of women and men, many of whom are employed in the local industry: tourism. She had thought that working in a styling salon would be more challenging, that she would learn from the expertise of fellow stylists and from the comments of her customers. She thought that because haircuts were twice the price she had charged in the previous barber shop, that her pay would be better. In both respects she was disappointed.

She tried to share some of her frustration with Cab, but he seemed unable to hear any words that might raise question about their, his, decision to move. He'd hated the east county, it's slowness and flatness. Fogies out there had no imagination and no guts. He'd even once said it was sexless country. That remark had stung Barbara, but she didn't know why she took it personally and so she said nothing. On the subject of haircutting, Cab said, "Sure you're not going to make any money working in someone else's salon. The point is to get your own clients, you see? Then you open your own business."

"I know, Cab," Barbara said.

"You're a beautiful, intelligent woman. People like you. You just have to sell yourself a little." He had been peeling the seal from a bottle of Merlot. He uncorked it. He had the efficiency of a machine.

"I know, Cab," she said.

"You've got to cut out the middle man."

"Like you? You're a middle man."

Cab poured himself a goblet. "And you're a funny woman," he said. He gave his wine a swirl, watched the syrupy legs run down the sides of the glass. "Hey, I'm not going to be doing what I'm doing forever." He walked into the next room, set the newspaper on his knees.

"Well, neither am I." Barbara paused in the doorway to touch the place where her bangs used to be. "I'm thinking I might rather cut animal's hair."

"What, like poodles?"

"I was thinking about sheep and goats."

Cab snapped a crease out of the business section. "I'll be happy if I never see another goddamn goat in my life," he said.

Joseph Brooder doesn't talk much. He is silent when he is angry and silent when he is sad. He gets annoyed by clutter and he shakes his head. He shakes his head at bad drivers. Once he nearly crushed a neighbor's collie with his pickup—crazy pup that barked night and day. He'd punched the breaks just in time and the impact was slight. The thing limped away, whelping, looking as if its feelings were hurt. Katja had been in the passenger seat. She put her hands to her chest and let out a scream. Joseph laughed. "Dumb, stupid dog," he said. It was a piercing laugh. "He'll learn. Stupid dog. He'll learn. That's how they learn."

Katja's insides froze.

"I learned something about our new neighbors." Barbara told Cab. "She's Russian from Russia."

"When did you talk to her?" Cab wanted to know.

"Oh, she popped into the salon today. She didn't get her hair cut, she was just checking things out, shopping in the neighborhood. She was very friendly. She said if there's ever anything we need, just drop by."

"She said that?"

"Sure Cab, it's called being neighborly."

"So what's she doing here?"

"She said she always wanted to live in America, and especially California, where," Barbara tilted her head down and looked through her eyelashes as she attempted a sultry Russian accent, "'anybody can make the life if she wants.'"

"How'd she meet whatshisname?"

"You won't believe it."

"I think I can guess, one of those mail order deals."

"That's not what she said. She said she met him at a dance in a place called Belgorod near her home."

"Well that's how they do it."

"That's not what she said, Cab."

"Well, what was he doing in Belgorod?"

"All she said was she knew she wanted," again the fluttering eyelashes and broken English, "'to be sharing the life with a serious man.'" Barbara could see that Cab was not amused by her imitation. She added flatly, "Joseph struck her as serious from the first moment she saw him."

"You can say that again."

"There's nothing wrong with serious."

"He takes checking his mailbox and watering his lawn pretty serious, too."

"Well, she didn't say anything about that."

"What else did she say?"

"She only just popped in. She didn't tell me her life story."

Cab is a free thinker, and he says that much of the unhappiness and animosity in the world is a result of people's fear of thinking freely. Even though he buys sofas, loveseats, and other mass-produced home furnishings, then marks them up for big profits, he can still think about being a socialist, which is what he thinks is best. Even though he's married to Barbara and loves her like a best friend, he can think about other women. He imagines that he could also choose not to think about other women, but that's never been his choice. He'd like to learn Katja Brooder's life story. He'd like to hear it from her. More than that, he'd like to open her silk robe and kiss her neck and her breasts.

Before he became a buyer, Cab was a salesman and he was well trained in what were called "communication skills." He learned to pause and listen, when to interrupt, how to flatter, how to use his hands and eyes to become suddenly confidential. In his college days, fifteen years ago, the hook of his nose and his big red shining ear lobes were his prominent features, no matter how he wore his dark brown hair. He didn't like it when people looked at his face. Now he thinks he wasted many years, but he also thinks his time has finally come. In spite of a penchant for gin and dollar cigars, Cab has aged well.

"He has serious potential," Barbara whispered to her friend, Dawn, the first day Cab walked into their barber shop. Cab asked Barbara where he might rest his leather briefcase, he admired some photos on the wall—pictures that Barbara had taken of "The Wind" near her home. He was the only customer ever to take a long look. "Strength," he said. "I see loneliness," he said. "You can't really see the wind," he smiled. Barbara might have argued the last point, but she was blushing and suddenly tongue-tied. Then, with his confidential look and tone, he described to her how he wanted his hair trimmed behind his ears. She was impressed by his clarity and self-assurance. He was impressed because she'd gotten it right. And there was something soothing in her touch. He would be passing frequently because he had clients in the next town. She would be chiding herself for waiting, but waiting, sometimes staring out the big plate glass front of the barber shop. Sometimes the wind brought surprises down Main Street.

*   *   *

Cab knocks and he waits. He holds his empty cup at crotch level. He raises it up to his chest. What am I really hoping for? What could possibly happen? He is sobering by the second. He tries to recover that light, breezy feeling.

Who could it possibly be? At the Smilie's house the phone is ringing. "Hello," says Barbara. She is answered by a click and a dial tone. She punches *69 and a woman picks up. "Hello," says the woman.

"Did you just call?" Barbara asks.

"No."

"Who are you?"

"Who are you?" says the woman. "I was calling for Cab."

"I'm Cab's wife."

"Oh," says the woman. Again, click and dial tone. Barbara walks through the house calling Cab.

Who could it possibly be? Katja is approaching the door and in spite of her heart, her mind fills with pictures of the man she loves. Her moments of longing for him are as unpredictable as he was. It couldn't possibly be him. He is in Belgorod or Novgorod or Vladisvlastock. He might be in prison or dead, or worse, married. But no, he is on a street corner playing his violin for rubles because he has to be, because that's how she left him more than five years ago. How could she still believe his silly promise to appear one day on her doorstep?

She believes. She is packed and ready.

Joseph finally finds his maul standing in a dark corner, but still no wedge. As he lifts it, his elbow tips and topples a sealed cardboard box. He hears the muffled sound of glass breaking. He is confused, almost paralyzed, before he takes a razor-knife from his workbench and cuts the tape from the package, opens it. Under layers of newspaper, then tissue, he finds one crystal candle stick holder and one broken partner. He also finds a photo of his Katja, hair down around her shoulders, wistful eyes. On the back of the photo are three Russian words he doesn't know. He nods, he mumbles, "I can open any goddamn box I like. This is my garage. This is my goddamn house." But he does not open any more boxes. With his right hand, he grips his sixteen pound maul around the neck. With his left, he slaps away some tools hanging from hooks on the wall that divides the garage from the kitchen. He steps back a half step and plants his feet. He heaves the big hammer up over his shoulder.

*   *   *

Joseph Brooder is wise enough to know that a part, a very big part, of what made him appealing to Katja Yurkina—age 27; height 160cm; weight 52kg; hair black; eyes brown; education higher; children no; etc.—was the lifestyle that he could provide her.

And for Katja, there had been a lover whom she loved, but he was not a serious man. He would never make the life for her. And there might have been others, Germans, Australians, Japanese, and Americans, sure, but so were there other girls, younger girls, so many and so hungry.

In Belgorod, Katja earned her master's degree in music history—specifically, eighteenth-century Russian folk music. What would she do in Joseph's little California resort town—the nearest university a junior college forty-five miles away? "Is OK with me," she told him in a gaudy, strobe-lit ballroom over an expensive glass of imported champagne. "I don't need work for to enjoy life." Dark, shining eyes and a thin curl in her brassy lips, she was stunning when she said it. It was what Joseph had wanted to hear, though he forgets sometimes, feels resentful sometimes. Sometimes in the dark loneliness of his garage he thinks, What a clever man I am, but other times he thinks, What do I need with a beautiful wife? And, Give me back my peace. There was an implicit bargain that should have been more explicit. Joseph would never say it, except alone in the dark garage stumbling over boxes of this and that extravagance: "You want credit cards. Well, dammit, I want, too."

In the early days of their marriage, he took pleasure in the looks he and Katja got when they went to Bertha's for a shrimp-boat, or down to George's Hideaway for vodka martinis and a couple of shots of Old Crow. Then he started looking harder at the looks. When she had looked at him with wonder and appreciation, when she swayed into him and slid her slender hand into his back pocket, they, young and old, men and women, looked upon invisible Joseph Brooder with wide eyes and open jaws. He liked it. When radiant Katja looked not at him, but into the faces in the long mirror behind the long bar, he didn't pause for hurt, nor did he feel enraged, not at least in a way that he was aware of. He returned to an old habit of mumbling and nodding to himself. He began training his eyes to see only what he must find.

In Minnesota, when Barbara was seventeen, her mother and father went to the country fair to evaluate some new model combines and tractors. They'd be gone overnight. There was always a big fuss before leaving the house. Barbara couldn't wait for them to go. "Don't you want to go?" They asked. "What are you going to do here all by yourself?" Her mother's parting words: "Do your homework. Don't mope. Clean your room. Behave." As he climbed into the truck, her father brushed back her hair with one of his swollen hands and with a face full of apology he merely said, "Take care of yourself."

It was rare for her to be alone in the sprawling ranch house.

She stood next to the telephone waiting, facing the big kitchen window. Outside showed nothing but green and yellow stalks of corn, a pulsing summer sky, and on the rise a mustard-colored barn. She felt on the cusp of sad and restless; she knew it could change in an instant. She chided herself for being so dependent upon someone else to make her happy.

Barbara was a large girl, not yet attractive to the boys her age. At school she was shy, walked the halls with her head low, hair hanging over her eyes. Among her friends she was known as a good listener; but with one friend, someone new and wild, also named Barbara, a girl from a county so far away that the weather was different, she found she could be herself, which often meant being very silly and sometimes deeply confidential. When the phone finally rang, Barbara pounced on it. "What took you so long? You're coming, right? Oh Barbara, I can't believe it. With him? I thought…it doesn't matter. I don't want to do it without you. This was our big chance. Let me stop." It really did feel as if her heart was sinking in her chest, and shrinking too. "You have a good time," she managed. "Don't do anything I wouldn't do."

In the silent house her own words echoed in her mind, "I wouldn't do." What ensued was a fierce internal debate: It's your own damn fault for being such a chickenshit. You'll always be lonely, vs. Damn the idiot boys, and damn Barbara for being just as stupid.

Be careful, little girl, said a comforting voice. Don't do anything foolish. She was not now standing in front of the phone or the big kitchen window, but by her desk in her bedroom. She opened the top drawer and removed an envelope from which she extracted one of two hits of blotter acid—the other had been for her girlfriend. She could hear her friend's advice: "It's not good to do it alone, not the first time. Don't do it if you're feeling depressed or anxious." And the other voice, "Be careful. Don't do anything…" she put the stamp on her tongue and chewed and swallowed "…I wouldn't do."

Within forty-five minutes Barbara's harsh self-approbation turned to panic. Her bedroom walls were papered with posters of skinny rock ikons in tight leather pants. They'd looked sexy to her, but this evening she could only see them as morbid, desperate. She wouldn't dare look at the Charles Manson biography she had been reading. She moved into the living room, slowly, cautiously touching the walls and doorframes. She was taken with the oak grain in the threshold—what it must have heard. Through her fingers she could hear the voices of her parents. Soon the entire house was alive with admonitions, imprecations, ridicule. Why don't you take some pride in your appearance? You mope around like an old goat. Hold your head up and smile. It's no wonder the boys...you'll never.... She'd put water on the stove for tea, something she thought would soothe her, but when the kettle screamed she was driven out into the yard.

She watched her big bare feet step after step on the dusty road, the evening air bristling her arms. The air was buzzing with life and blurring with vibrant color. She would not look up, not think about the demons hiding in the green stalks, an ontogeny of evil. There had been the Grumpus—an invention of her grandfather's to keep a little girl from getting herself lost in the corn—cum dragon, cum snake, cum beady-eyed farm hand with a metal rake to comb the flesh from her bones. A simple walk to the barn had turned into a howling odyssey. "Breathe," she told herself. "Don't panic. Breathe." And the first time she breathed deeply she felt better. The next time she dared to look up. She could not separate her own breath, the air she pulled in and out, from the wind that tittered the tops of the cornstalks. With one big blow she pushed the electric clouds across the sky.

She entered the barn where Nifty brushed his flanks against the panels of his stall. Nifty had given a good hard kick at everyone who'd ever gotten close to him, even broke one of the farm hand's ribs. But never Barbara. Her mother and father said she had a way with him. She wondered how he might react to her in her hypervigilant state. Nifty nodded, pressed his huge face into her armpit, kissed her fingers. His breath was warm and sweet. Big and strong, beautiful Nifty, she brushed and combed and patted and kissed him. She stood at his side until her feet ached, until she could only see blackness through the gap in the barn door.

What a trip! To think that it's my own mind that filled the cornfield with monsters. And that I could fill it with different stuff, and… She lit a lantern and she gathered a couple of Nifty's wool blankets. She hugged her knees in the hayloft. Big Barb, as she was known at school, cradled herself for warmth. Her hands stroked her long, strong arms, her round, muscular shoulders, her thick knees, the hips she despised. Between exhaustion and sleep she made many resolutions, most of which she forgot in the hazy week that followed; but she'd remember the secret name she'd given to her new incarnation: California.

California is big and beautiful. California is tolerant. California is a place where anything can happen and anyone can be whoever she wants.

Twelve years young, Joseph Brooder had found a box of magazines in his father's garage. "You don't disturb my things, boy," his father had warned. Joe Sr. had no idea how much his things would disturb his son. The mysteries of adulthood made the boy ache. It was ugly to think of women that way: that triangle of fur; those bland, hungry eyes; the pink or brown nipples turned in or out or up that seemed to have an expression of their own. Nothing had ever pushed and pulled him so at the same time, except for the contents of the box beneath the box of magazines. In it Joseph found his father's pistol. Black and steel and smooth; how could something so small be so heavy? The gravity of the gun made him feel weak, like in love.

One day Joseph was found with his pants around his knees, stroking his bare thighs with the stem of the pistol. He was beaten until he bled from his backside. Worse than that, he became a stranger to his mother and father.

Nowadays, Joseph keeps his own secrets in his own garage, a mumbled litany of desire and frustration. But what is all this goddamn clutter?

*   *   *

When Katja opens the door, there stands Cab holding his empty cup in front of his hooked nose, peering into it. He fills his lungs and smiles his winningest, but his eyes are narrow to study her first response. "Howdy neighbor," he says. "Good morning," he says. He spies the disappointment on her face and it causes him to stammer. "I was, um, wondering," he says, before he is interrupted by the dull clap of steel against plywood and the subsequent crash of glass and china on the kitchen floor. The sound seems to be coming from the garage. Katja reels back into the house. A second thudding blow sends a clock across the room, its face shatters against the stove. The third and fourth cracks of the maul make thin faultlines in the kitchen plaster. Cab steps into the threshold, pauses. Katja screams and then folds in upon herself on the floor. The fifth blow breaks through the wall, jagged splinters in a cloud of white dust.

"Cab?" Barbara calls from their front door. Barefoot, she paces the black path, glimpses her husband passing through the neighbor's doorway. She walks faster, passes the open garage and sees Joseph Brooder, now leaning on the handle of his maul, shuddering. She says, "Hello," and he nods and continues to nod, but probably not at her. She carries on toward the sound of the woman weeping. When she reaches the doorway, Cab and Katja are coming out of the house arm in arm, Katja's face is shrouded by one of her hands.

"What's going on?" Barbara asks Cab.

"I don't know," says Cab. He leads Katja down the path toward his house. Neither of them look at Barbara. Cab looks vaguely in the direction of Joseph Brooder, says, "You're sick, buddy. I feel sorry for you." Brooder's upper lip recedes, baring his teeth, but he doesn't move. Cab turns his attention back to Katja's hand, like a broken lark, folded in his own.

Barbara follows them a few steps, then, "What's going on, Cab?"

And again, "I don't know."

"Well, what are you doing here?"

"For to borrow something?" Katja says, trying to catch her breath.

"Borrow what?"

"Is it important?" Cab says. "Sugar!"

Barbara looks down at her bare feet on the black path, then up at her neighbor in the shadow of his garage. He looks like one recovering from a seizure, still, except for the twitching in his back and elbows. He sags over the handle of his maul. "We have sugar," she says. "A full bag," her voice trailing off. She takes one step and then another toward Joseph. Katja turns away from Cab to look. Cab turns too.

What can they see? You can't see the wind, not really, only what it moves. You can't see pain either, only Barbara leaning into it, her fingertips now brushing the hair behind Joseph's ear, Joseph lowering his heavy head onto her shoulder.

Mr. Passion

"SAY SOMETHING?" BRENDA SAYS. She changes Billy's diaper. "Ba boom ba boom," she sings for distraction. Eight months old, Billy hates to lie flat on his back.

I skim the Sunday *Press Democrat*. News is bleak and so am I. Nothing sticks lately but boredom. "Misery, I said. Woe unto us." I don't know why I feel so spent. I open the wood stove and set a log of bay on the cinders. It sizzles. "All is vanity and vexation of spirit," I say, mock thunder in my voice.

"Uh oh. Time for the Sunday sermon," Brenda says. "Ba boom." Rain blows hard against the plexiglass skylight. Twigs brush the tile roof and water spills from a rusted hole in the spout. "Get the pacifier, Honey?" Brenda calls from the baby's bedroom. She nurses Billy in a recliner and with her free hand pops in a cassette, "Little Jackie Rabbit." Billy's eyes roam as his lids slowly fall. I find the pacifier under a pink and blue shawl in the crib.

Brenda lifts Billy off her breast and together we make the quick transition to the rubber nipple. He's down.

"Ready?" Brenda asks. I woke with a hard-on and all morning I've been ready. I want to fuck so badly it hurts, but fucking is not on the agenda.

"Yes." I pull my sweatshirt up over my head.

"To do the exercises," Brenda says.

"I know." Recently Brenda brought home a book called *Sexual Healing* to help us enjoy sex again. Since Billy was born it has been hard for Brenda to relax. We feel so new at this parenting business. Brenda and I are in our mid-thirties and until eight months ago we enjoyed such freedom our friends were envious. We each lived alone and came and went as we pleased. Brenda is a half-time nurse at a nearby health clinic. I am an art student and I work on-call at The Open Door, a sixty-day homeless shelter. I had earned enough to feel secure and to do the things I like most—camping with Brenda, biking with Brenda, sipping Merlot on Brenda's porch, reading stories together, sleeping in, making love.

Now the future is an unpaved road before us. It beckons but demands vigilance as we go. Brenda worries. Shopping lists of anxiety: is there lead in our paint? iron in Billy's cereal? fluoride in our water? meaning in our lives? It is hard for her to feel sexually excited and harder still to sustain such feeling with the constant fear of interruption.

I worry, too. Have I lost my touch? My art projects are lifeless hodge-podges of broken glass and china in clay. "Fragmented," I'm told in school. "Unfocused." I've begun to lose my sense of purpose at The Open Door, often seeking refuge behind the closed door of the office. Life is endless toil and even sex feels like work, anxious to get it right, too anxious to enjoy.

We begin the exercises with five minutes of spoon breathing as we have on other days, to be followed by ten minutes of frontal caress, and today according to the book, we're ready to start with ten minutes of genital caress. We're undressed under the cotton comforter. I try to concentrate on breathing with Brenda. A ticking in the wood stove signals that the catalytic converter is kicking in, but the room still feels cold and damp. From Billy's bedroom I can hear *"Little Jackie Rabbit has a funny habit…"*

"Want to go first?" Brenda whispers.

"Sure, I'll start." With a precision that feels religious I fold back the comforter to Brenda's bare hips. She pulls it back up to her navel.

"I'm cold," she smiles and squeezes her shoulders.

"OK," I say. This part should be relaxing, but I feel heat spreading through the hollow in my chest. I breathe. Propped on my left elbow I begin with my right hand lightly stroking from the base of Brenda's throat to the arc of her breasts. I like the way her nipples turn out. Her eyes are closed and her jaw is taut. My hand seems to have its own mind. *Concentrate on the point of contact,* the book says. It promises to take us to *higher levels of feeling.* My hand turns at the wrist, fingers gently opening and closing like the bristles of a soft brush cutting an intricate cornice.

"Don't touch my nipples yet," Brenda says. "Please."

"I didn't."

"I know."

"You're supposed to relax," I say, shrillness leaking in.

"I'm trying," Brenda says. Billy makes a brief yelp. We know the sound. The pacifier has probably slipped out of his mouth.

"If you're trying to control this thing, you're not doing the exercise right," I say. I feel pathetic saying it. Doesn't she want me, on her, in her, as close as we can be? We could laugh and cry out loud. We could forget all our worries, forget the fucking world.

"You're right," she says. "Go slowly." My cock curls against my thigh. There's thin gratification in being right. I begin again at her throat and brush down between her breasts to her navel where my fingers play at widening circles. Four fingertips surf the crest of her collarbone and ride out to the faded tan line on her shoulder and down and I wonder what I'm choking back. Let my hand think. Whispering up the crevasse beneath her right breast and circling and closing in, I close my eyes and struggle to find feelings of tenderness. I trace the soft inflections of her inner elbow down to her wrist.

"That's nice," she says.

"Sshh." I'm grateful and resentful. I don't want instructions.

And I don't need a goddamn handbook because I know how to make love. It wasn't so long ago that Brenda was bent at the waist, her palms pressing the arm of the sofa, my hands tight around the cheeks of her ass while I thrust in and in and out as fast as our panting together. I need to concentrate again on the touch, the point of contact. *Don't think about performance*, the book says. *Don't think.*

But there were others before Brenda. Angela with dreadlocks. She would nearly convulse, her head like a mop shaking on the end of a pole. She moaned like a feral cat and she bleated, "Fuck me, ooh, please, ooh, fuck me," so that even I, Mr. Passion, felt a shudder of embarrassment. Now as I caress Brenda's hip and hesitantly bend back the tips of her pubic hair, I long for Angela whom I never even liked.

"That tickles," Brenda says. I stroke the inside of her kneecap, down her calf and squeeze the arch of her foot.

"It's your turn," I say. I roll onto my back. My cock is stiff again. It pokes in the air, and I remember licking circles around Brenda's clitoris. Her hips rolling, unfurling. She flag. Me pole. I'd mount her then. Love was our homeland and we'd seize it with righteous force.

"Are you comfortable?" Brenda asks.

"Yes." It was never my intention to dominate *her*. I wanted for us to conquer together. Surrender together. I want now. I want so much so bad it hurts. I'm not asking for different, higher levels of feeling. I liked what we had. I never ask for too much. In most respects I'm self-sufficient. I'm proud of my humility. I don't need to be right. Rarely do I feel troubled when Brenda gives recommendations: how to get the laundry cleaner; how to fasten Billy's diaper more securely; how to stack kindling; where to hang wet towels; when to change the oil in my Charger—the Dodge would be in a junkyard now if it weren't for Brenda's ministrations—and though I should concentrate on her touch, the list goes on; don't smoke in the house; don't wipe the floor with that; don't leave the doors open in this cold and damp. I've been counting and resenting since we began these awful exercises. I should concentrate, but I've never had to carry these *shoulds* into bed.

She begins at the base of my throat. I feel her hand like a breath across my chest. Fifteen years ago I had plenty to learn about making love. *Focus.* My first girlfriend could have been a coach with a clipboard and a whistle. *Focus, the point of contact.* Stop. Go slow. Now here. Faster. No, not there. But I loved her, or I thought I did. I thought that was what love was supposed to feel like, and then without warning one day the feeling was gone.

Brenda and I intend to share our lives together and so I believe we'll make it work. I feel her hand pass over the tuft of hair below my beltline and fan out along the top of my right thigh. It's her breast, I think, that knocks against the head of my penis—that buoy awash in currents of desire.

"I'm sorry," she says.

"I like it."

"We're not there yet."

I sit up, my elbows behind me. Our eyes meet. Her mouth is an inch from the tip of my cock and when she talks I feel her breath electric. Her eyes go wide and sad and soft. A flashflood of worry and sympathy.

"What's wrong?"

"Nothing," I say. The word "entitled" comes to mind. Some small corner of my brain sees how ridiculous I am and wants to laugh, but cannot.

"Try to relax." She brushes her hand down my outer thigh, my knee, my calf and she squeezes my foot. I can't relax. With every moment, every breath, I want to be held, squeezed, swallowed. I slide out of Brenda's grasp.

"Can't do this," I mutter, walking to the bathroom. I close the door. With the faucet running I watch my face contort in the mirror. A forgotten wrinkle twitches the corner of my lips. A shiver. Pathetic. Brenda lightly taps on the door.

"You OK?" I pretend not to hear because I don't want to show my face or speak through my hollowness. My cock is still poking out, clueless, like a hand expecting to be shaken.

"Hey," she says, and pushes the door open a few inches. "Oh Sweetie," she says. Billy rattles the bars of his crib and roars and I can't hold back my tears any longer. Brenda hugs me and strokes my cheeks with hers, warm and wet. "I can make you feel better," she says.

"I know," I say. "I can do it myself. But not now." I feel frustration turn to anger, turn again to shame and now something else, raw hurt. The point of contact? I seem stuck with hurt. "We better let the little tiger out," I say.

"I'll get him," Brenda says. She kisses me and assures me. "It's going to work," she says. She looks hard at my face for a response. I study the soap dish, then the shower curtain. "It's going to work," she says. She takes her plaid robe off a hook on the back of the door and wraps it around herself. In a moment Billy's roaring gives way to whimpering and then soft cooing. I grab a pair of sweat pants off the hamper and the T-shirt hanging from the handle of the vacuum cleaner. It's purple and it has the old Nehi logo on the chest. It's my oldest piece of clothing. I wore it in high school and in college and I was wearing it the day Billy was born. I've seen some changes in that shirt.

From the living room table I gather my pouch of tobacco, papers, a lighter and the front pages of the *Press Democrat*. The porch feels wet and cold on my bare feet, but I'm glad to be outside breathing bigger air. I roll my cigarette and fire it up. I happen to open to the page of the news where I'd left off—woe and misery—a story about child sweatshops in Ceylon.

Children, says the paper, are shackled to tables, made to work fourteen and fifteen hours a day, paid the equivalent of a U.S. quarter. They are beaten. They are exposed to toxins. Their open sores get infected. Horrible as it all is, I can't feel it. I'm only seeing black boxes on a flat white page until I'm taken by a photograph of a girl and her baby goat seated by the side of an unpaved road. *Seven-year-old beggar*, reads the caption. They are wrapped together in a frayed and dusty shawl. I can see the ridges of the goat's ribs through the fur on its back. The goat looks at the girl, its nose against her chin. The girl is looking at me. Her eyes are blacker than any black on the page—then they aren't on the page. They breathe, they hover, they want so much, so badly, that they have traveled half way around the world to find me here, full of pity.

White Veil

TY'S HAND LIES FLAT, HIS FINGERS EXTEND above the steering wheel dividing the dull white sky into parts. "One thing's for sure," he says distractedly, not with his usual enthusiasm.

"What?" Lucy's also distracted. Exhausted. She'd been watching the rows of corn, and the empty spaces at seventy miles per hour. She'd like to comb her hair and searches the glove compartment for a comb, but finds a stick of sugarless gum instead. Her chewing disrupts the pleasant illusion, the long straight lines which appear to funnel open and zip shut, but soon the movement of her jaw creates its own somnolent rhythm. "What one thing?" she asks. "Do you want a piece of gum?"

"I want aspirin," Ty says, "or a Bloody Mary."

"That sounds good."

"Which one?"

"What's it like another hour to the cottage?" The cottage on the lake had been rented by Ty's parents for the honeymoon. Ty's parents honeymooned there thirty years ago. Lucy's parents did not attend the wedding. Her mother died in a collision and her father confessed that the ceremony would only make her absence more poignant. Lucy combs her long hair with her fingers.

"It was a helluva party," says Ty, "that's for sure."

"Huh," Lucy'd been breathing shallowly. She sighs. She'd had her hands curled on her thighs. She opens and closes them.

"I told you they'd go for Mom's lasagna."

Lucy brightens. "Six trays, plus the pot roast, plus the scalloped potatoes. The marigolds were a nice touch, don't you think? The table looked beautiful, don't you think?"

"They pigged out," says Ty. "And the beer. Two whole kegs before midnight. That's gotta be a record. I'd've had more myself if the old man hadn't insisted on shots of Tequila."

"You guys," Lucy says. No anger in her voice, a soft chiding. "Any excuse to get obliterated." She turns back to the zipping corn.

Some of the jokes had been awful. Ty as in tying the knot. As Ty was buttoning his suit, he'd said, "Fit to be tied." How many times had she heard that one? "Hog-tied." And "Could Loose Lucy be tied down?" Loose Lucy was especially not funny, like calling an obese man Tiny. She had been more prudent than her girlfriends. She'd had only one lover before Ty, a gentle, sullen young man who'd devoted his life to the priesthood. That had been winter and this is the middle of July, sunflowers as big as your head. She's forgotten his silence, the icy-cold black puddles and hot tears, remembers only that she wanted to feel devoted, too. No more suffering visionaries, she'd said, and no more heartbreaks. Ty is a drummer in a marching band.

"It was a helluva party."

"When I was five years old." Lucy's voice trails off. She doesn't notice the car slowing until Ty crosses onto the shoulder and she hears tinging tar pebbles in the wheel wells.

"Nature calls," Ty says. He moves differently in his pleated slacks and starched shirt. Maybe it's the leather Florsheims. She'd grown accustomed to his high-top sneakers or bare feet, but she likes this look. He has always exuded confidence, but now so handsome, almost dignified. He walks around the front of the car and stands a foot behind Lucy's door. "...I dreamed of my wedding day," Lucy whispers. There were to be marigolds, and there were, but only Lucy noticed them. There were to have been rose petals sprinkled from a wicker basket onto the nuptial path. Ty visited "countless" florists but none would sell him petals from their old roses. Ty opens his trousers and thrusts his hips forward. Lucy turns in her seat so that she can see his back. My husband. How many times has she thought it and when will it sink in? His shoulders look unusually broad. Why has he thrust his hips so far forward? It isn't windy. A still white sky. He looks as if he is preparing to dance the limbo. Limbo under the torch-lights in the backyard. Ty holding the collar of his jacket and slinging it. She can still hear the whistling and Ty's best friend who laughs like a horse. So much hooting before the boys finally packed it in.

"You heard what my mother was saying last night?" Ty starts the engine.

"No, what?"

"She said the cottage on the lake is haunted."

"No."

"She did. But you know my mother. She believes what she reads in the check-out lines. She's gullible as you can get." Ty laughs. "She married my old man."

Lucy feels something coming on, like carsickness, but more sudden, a wave of anxiety. Maybe she left something burning on a stove somewhere. Ty doesn't worry—so goes the lore of his family and friends. That's what you gotta love about Ty. He doesn't dwell on problems—he calls 'em as he sees 'em, then moves on. Once, only once, Lucy shared some of the details of her previous relationship. "Everybody gets jilted sometime, honey," Ty said. "At least you got jilted for God," he laughed.

"I've never been scared of ghosts," says Ty. "Now werewolves give me the creeps. The way they get their claws in your skin. And those fangs." Ty shows his upper teeth. "Even scarier than a nagging wife," he laughs. "You're not going to be that kind of wife, are you?"

Lucy tries to laugh, but can't. She feels an urge to cry, but can't. She'd cried at the wedding. She hadn't cried like that since she was a little girl. But brides always cry at their weddings, they're supposed to. Had she heard about the ghost? No. She'd deliberately avoided Ty's mother. Dark circles, chain-smoking, cackling laugh, there'd be plenty of opportunities to know the woman better, but not on her wedding day. How then does she see this image—a wisp of a woman in a lacy white veil. Maybe the ghost that frightened Ty's mother did not wear a lacy white veil. It doesn't matter. Lucy's not gullible. She doesn't believe in ghosts.

"What's it another hour?" Her eyes are dry and fixed on the empty spaces.

A Day at the Beach

FRANCES STRETCHED HER BARE ARMS under the hot midday sun on a Widow's Walk in Cape May, New Jersey. She exhaled *ahh* to the breaking surf, the gulls, the misty sea air. The last time she had visited Cape May she was six years old. She had stayed with her Aunt Sal and Uncle Dan several blocks from the room she and Eve were now renting. She remembered finding dozens of spotted sandy brown frogs under the porch and she remembered the yellow plastic shovel she used to corral a frog into her hand to show to her uncle.

Eve unpacked. She savored unpacking, setting a stack of fresh cotton T-shirts and khaki shorts in the top drawer of a pine dresser, and she savored the first step onto the deck into the sunshine beside Frances. Eve frets and savors. She eats her string beans and her biscuit and saves her bites of grilled salmon for last. She strode slowly, luxuriously, on her slender feet into the ocean when she felt that she could not bear the heat any longer, that she and the ocean could no longer resist one another. She watched as the glistening surf mixed with the oil on her ankles and calves, silvery and supple. Frances ran, not like a woman of fifty, but like a six-year-old girl, into the crashing waves until she was knocked off her feet.

SNOWY TRUCKSTOP

Frances rolled off the turnpike for a cup of coffee to warm her hands and for a moment to rest her eyes from the blinding snow. She had made this drive easily thirty times from New York City to her parents' home in Delaware. She parked next to a Tortoise-shell Celica that shook and coughed white smoke. Inside the car, Frances saw a woman with short, dark brown hair, a thin, straight nose, a funny birdlike face. The woman turned the key and pumped the gas pedal furiously.

"You're going to flood it," Frances said, knocking on the woman's steamy window. Eve punched the steering wheel, accidentally sounding the horn. Frances waited. Eve rolled down her window, her dark eyes wet from crying.

"You're going to flood it."

"I don't care," Eve said. "I'm not sitting in this fuck-ing truckstop all night." Eve enunciated the ing part of "fucking."

Frances reached in and squeezed Eve's cold knuckles. "Come have coffee with me."

"Fuck-ing Celica."

"Let her rest," Frances couldn't help laughing. "I've got cables. We'll try to jump it after a coffee."

"I'm in a hurry," Eve said, fastened to her steering wheel.

"I'm not."

THE EMPTY NEST

Eve and Robert were quietly terrified of the day their daughter would go away to college. "Of course you're scared," said Eve's friend, Glenda, at the publishing company. "You'll be alone together, but you'll get through it. You'll like it. You must have loved each other once." Eve tried hard to remember.

Once before they were married, Eve sat awkwardly on the handlebars of a bicycle as Robert pedaled down the boardwalk. With all her squirming, he couldn't steer and they collided with a tandem bike going the opposite way. The other couple was very gracious. Eve and Robert laughed hard about it, then they tried again. Eve sat on the seat, her hands on Robert's hips, as he pedaled. For almost nineteen years Eve savored that memory like the last bite on her plate when all the flavor had gone out of everything else. She had crafted it over the years though, and when she permitted herself she could recall her strange reluctance to touch him. He was her lover and would be her husband, but she never felt intimacy. The awkwardness, the strangeness never went away, only the laughter.

Eve had anticipated the day she'd see a note on the formica topped dishwasher where she and Robert left each other messages: "Something's missing, Honey. I haven't been happy for as long as I can remember." She hadn't expected that she'd be the one to write it.

FROG LEGS

"He peed in my hand, Uncle Dan," said Franny. Uncle Dan rinsed sand off his feet with a hose beside the old wood-shingle beach house.

"Here," he said, pulling Franny by the wrist into the cool stream of water. "It's a frog. My goodness, won't that make a nice dinner?"

Franny ran from her uncle back under the porch. She was so upset that she forgot she held the frog in her hand and she squeezed the life out of it.

ON THE WIDOW'S WALK

Frances put her arm around Eve's shoulders and let it slide down until her hand found a place in the back pocket of Eve's shorts. They rested their tall tinkling gin and tonics on a two-by-four railing which surrounded the deck. Frances pulled Eve close, but Eve, meeting eyes with a boy in flip-flops outside the liquor store down below, pulled back.

"I'm uneasy," she said, tilting her head in the direction of the boy. The boy wore a T-shirt, his long, thin, red arms poking out of the holes where the sleeves had been ripped off. She couldn't make out all of the words printed on the shirt, but she could read *PUSSY*. The boy grabbed the arm of his skinny, bare-chested friend and they looked up at Eve and Frances on the Widow's Walk.

"Did I tell you I kissed a dead frog?" Frances said.

"And now you want to kiss me?"

"I must have kissed it one hundred times."

"Charming."

"Princess Charming," Frances added brightly.

A man stepped out of a maroon Camaro about fifty feet from the entrance to the liquor store. The bare-chested boy beckoned the man with a wave of his hand. Frances rubbed lotion from her pale instep to her broad, freckled knee. Eve watched as the boy in the T-shirt dug into the pockets of his shorts and handed a bill to the man. The bare-chested boy watched Eve watching. After the man walked into the liquor store, the boy turned and lowered his trunks, flashing Eve with his skinny, white buttocks.

"I see you've made a friend already," Frances said. Eve, looking away from the boy, saw a patrol car rolling slowly down the block. Perhaps it was the whiteness of the boy's butt, white as a baby's, or perhaps it was the memory of trying to get college students to buy beer for her and her friends more than three decades ago in Greenwich Village; Eve didn't know why, but she felt compelled to warn the boys that the police were coming.

Indiscreetly she pointed to the patrol car, drawing the attention of the cops first to herself, then to the boys. Frances stepped inside to get more ice for their drinks. Eve followed, but not without first being flipped off by one of the boys. The man, now exiting the store, looked first at the boys, then at the police, then at Eve who wished she were invisible.

LESS THAN LADYLIKE

When Frances was a sophomore at NYU studying the Romantic

poets, she found she had little patience for the ephemerality of words. Ideas are OK, but beauty has weight and substance. She experimented with drawing, painting, collage, and then she discovered sculpture. Her first completed piece was a block of steel two feet high. "This is real!" she said, kicking it with her leather work boots.

She was not at all troubled by the long looks people gave her when she was rigged in her overalls and carried her welder's mask on the Subway. She liked holding a blow-torch in her hand and she liked to think about breathing a little fire into the daily deadpan on the uptown train. If ever she felt a flicker of self-consciousness about her rough exterior or about holding hands with a girlfriend on the sidewalk, she needed only to remind herself that she was well protected and that she was in the business of creating something beautiful.

Choosing A Pair Of Shorts

"When the hell are we going to hit the beach?" Frances hollered. "And why for once can't you be in a good mood when I'm in a good mood."

"I'm in a good fuck-ing mood," Eve said. She tossed a pair of khaki shorts onto the bed and held a pair of black ones up to her waist in front of a mirror. "Do my legs look fat?"

"I can't believe this. Christ."

"They do look fat."

"Yep."

"They won't let me on the beach."

"Probably not."

"I'm worried, Fran."

"You're shaped like a fucking Flamingo."

"Not about that."

Frances shook her head. She picked her flip-flops off the floor and stuffed them into a canvas bag with two towels, lotion, and a couple of magazines. She zipped the bag and slung the straps over her broad shoulder.

"OK," Eve said.

"OK."

"Fix me another drink."

On the boardwalk a breeze caught a stack of napkins from the counter of a french-fry booth. They swirled and tripped along until each hit an obstacle: the side of a garbage can, the base of a public telephone, a little girl's waist, the back of Eve's ankle. She was startled by the touch.

Something about untied high-top sneakers, heavy metal T-shirts, bleached hair and baked eyes made Eve anticipate violence. The sun was hot, but when the breezes blew, she shivered. Frances breathed in and stretched her arms as wide as she could. "Ahh, to be out of the city." Eve smiled a limp smile. Fifty feet ahead on the boardwalk by the Skee-ball machines she saw the boy who hours before had flipped her off. Frances took Eve's hand in hers and squeezed it.

"How about a game of Skee-ball. I was Skee-ball Queen in my early days."

"I don't feel like playing," Eve said.

"Just one game."

"Let's go home." A cloud passed before the sun and a breeze sent the napkins swirling again. Eve took her hand out of Frances' and folded her arms.

"Come on. Just one game, or are you afraid I'll beat you?"

"Yes," Eve said. She turned and walked back toward their rented room. Frances stood in the center of the boardwalk. She'd been looking forward to an ocean getaway for a long time. Fresh air and the wide expanse of the sea, room to be as big as you want to be.

A FRIEND

When Eve gave birth to her daughter, Liza, Robert was out of town on a business trip. The doctor whom she'd gotten to know over months of prenatal check-ups had been suddenly called away for a family emergency. Eve overheard some words exchanged between the resident-in-charge and her nurse; "slim-hipped," "tense muscles," "incision." She had taken something for pain, but it seemed nothing could reduce her fear. The nurse, a roundish woman with sparkling green eyes, moved to Eve's bedside and held Eve's hand. When her eyes were closed, Eve still saw the glow of the overhead light, and in it a pair of soft green lights and a smile that sustained her.

LIQUID STEEL

When her kid brother, Louis, returned from Vietnam, Frances picked him up at the base in New York. She'd read all she could about the war, watched the TV news every day, and she didn't think she had any false expectations. Like her mother and father, she felt blessed that Louis was coming home alive.

Louis was quiet. Before they set out for Delaware, Frances wanted to buy him a beer, to sit and talk, but he declined. He'd come around, Frances thought. The wipers on Frances' Ranchero were inadequate against the torrents of rain. She pulled off the Turnpike and together they waited in the parking lot of a Howard Johnson's.

"Have a cheeseburger," Frances said.

"No. No thank you." Louis rubbed his knuckles on the window to clear away the fog and gaze at an empty stretch of pavement.

"Did Mom tell you about her new diet?" Frances laughed. "Grapefruits and popcorn. Makes your mouth water, doesn't it?"

"Yeah."

"And Dad's got a new toy. A snow blower. When he straps that thing on his back and puts on his big boots, he looks like he's off on a recon mission."

"Yeah."

"Ruthie got married and divorced. She'll be real happy to see you, kid."

"Rain's letting up," Louis said.

"OK," Frances rubbed her hands together, "Let's get going."

"Yeah."

"I guess you saw some terrible stuff over there."

"Doesn't seem to matter, Fran."

"You're here. That's what matters."

"Remember the tree fort?"

"Never mind that." But Frances had been thinking about it. When Louis was thirteen his best friend, Rob, drowned in the Country Club swimming pool. Louis and Rob had built a tree fort with plywood scraps and two-by-fours in the woods behind Rob's house. Frances made curtains for the fort and helped attach a tire swing to one of the tree's limbs. Louis and Rob spent entire weekends without leaving the fort. The only person they would permit to join them was Frances, and even she had to call out from twenty yards away where the path split in two.

Louis walked home from Rob's funeral despite his mother's insistence that he ride in the car. A few hours later, when the family was preparing to have dinner, Frances walked to the fort where she knew she'd find Louis. As she neared the woods behind Rob's house, she smelled smoke. By the time she reached the point where the paths divided, a thick black cloud had risen to the top of the tallest trees. She ran down the path. A flaming sheet of plywood crashed against the dirt and an explosion of sparks lit the ground. Louis, still dressed in his black suit, picked at the crease in his trousers. Sirens could be heard in the distance. Frances pulled on Louis' tie. "Mom and Dad are waiting for you." She led him out of the woods like a puppy on a leash.

"Yeah, I remember the tree fort," Frances said after a long, wet stretch of highway. "We had some good times in there."

"I guess so. I only remember that I couldn't go back to it after

Robbie died."

"Well, you made sure of that." Frances laughed and gave Louis a soft punch on the knee.

"I did." He stared out at the Jersey marshland and what appeared to be the rusty frame of a ferris wheel half sunken in mud.

A week later Frances got a phone call in New York from her father in Delaware. "Louis swerved off the highway into the base of an overpass. He's dead. No one else was hurt. Can you come home soon, Fran?" She didn't remember deciding. No, it hadn't been a choice she'd made consciously, but somehow she'd prepared herself for this news.

THE WINDOW GARDEN

With a pencil Eve poked five holes into the dirt in her window box. She dropped a couple of dill seeds into each of the holes about a quarter inch deep. When the green sprigs reached the top of her small window frame, she'd decide whether or not to live with Frances. And if the dill didn't take, she'd try basil. And if the basil failed, rosemary. At fifty years of age, she felt like a girl again.

CLOSE TO HOME

Several blocks from their rented room, Eve and Frances walked along quietly. Eve switched her magazine from under her right arm to under her left and locked her elbow in Frances's. The sky was dark, the sidewalk narrow and lined with birch trees.

A low rumbling could be heard just beyond the corner. A car approached, and the sound became higher and louder. Eve recognized the maroon Camaro and the driver recognized Eve. The car backed down the block and stopped several feet from the two women.

Inside the car was dark, but Eve could see a thick, red arm resting on the driver's door. The shoulder bore a tattoo: a hand grenade expanding as if beginning to explode.

"Fucking dykes," said the head behind the big arm. Eve could feel him staring at her even though she couldn't see his eyes. She stood with one hand on a birch trunk and the other arm wrapped around Frances. With her eyes closed she heard a heartbeat she thought was her own. The ground beneath her seemed to give way like sand being pulled in an undertow. After a minute of painful silence, the car screeched forward and out of sight. Eve opened her eyes and found Frances standing beside her, solid as a steel sculpture.

"Dammit," said Frances rinsing their glasses in the sink. "I forgot to get tonic."

"Straight gin will be fine." Eve sat on the bed in her under-pants. She touched the pink flesh of her thigh and watched it change to white, and back to pink. Frances entered the room with two icy glasses.

"You have legs like a bird."

"A fat bird," Eve said. "And you kiss dead frogs."

Frances nodded. One tear and then another streamed down her cheek and cooled on her upper lip. She couldn't remember the last time she'd felt tears. Hadn't it been at this beach? All her impulses told her to wipe them away but someone was squeezing her hands with a strength equal to her own.

Toxic Round-up

TOO MANY COOKS. TOO MANY CHIEFS. Too many transmissions shifting out of sync. Too many hands in the air. Too many new releases. Too much desperation. There are good germs and bad germs, but too many surfaces. Too many drugs to choose from. Too many missiles, spears, bullets, words. Not enough targets. Too many choices of coffee makers. Too many shoes in the closet.

I found a clearing on a hillside. Nothing there.

There are too many punchlines, not enough ways to fold your hands at a funeral. Too many condolences. Too many rhymes with love. Too many signs at the supermarket. Too many symptoms of heart disease. Too much noise, way too much noise.

I was out driving—what I do to get away—what I do. I met her at the annual Toxic Round-up. I'm a sucker for a woman in a mylex suit. "Too many yardsales," I said.

"Too many toxins," she added. "Not enough buckets."

"I know a clearing," I said. "It's on a hillside."

"Too many trees," she said. "Children behind every tree. Too many forms of hide and seek."

"Not enough finding," I said.

"Yes," she said, "too much not enough." She asked me not to get out of my car.

"What do you do?" I said.

"I do what I'm doing," she said. "Too often."

"And you," she asked. "Shut off your engine," she said. "Too many engines."

"I drive," I said.

"Too many cars."

"Too many pedestrians," I added. "Too many gridlocks. Not enough keys."

"I'm with you," she said. "One hundred percent."

"You are? What part? What did I say?"

"Come see us again," she said. "Be sure to bring waste." She waved me on.

II

I met her again a year later. Too long to wait. Buckets in my hatchback: used paint thinner, cement thinner, termite thinner.

"Don't get out of your car," she said, "too many people do."

"I wouldn't," I said. "Why would I?"

"I remember you. Mr. Curious."

"Don't you get hot in that plastic coverall?" I asked. "Sweat trickling underneath?"

"That'll do," she said. "That'll more than do."

"I know a clearing in the woods. Quiet as death."

"I have a root cellar," she said. "Some empty jars there. A centipede. Nothing more."

"Want to see my scar?" I said. "I've had things removed." She took out a yellow flag and waved me forward to the red tarpaulin.

The sky is crowded with satellites, signals, invisible images, and inaudible noises. At any given moment, the soles of six hundred and forty Florsheims may pass overhead. Lunches in plastic compartments, polystyrene cups with logos, magazines, chewing gum, headsets, in short, humanity fills the air. It burrows, swims, crawls, walks, jumps, and flies. But time doesn't fly, not anymore. There were three hundred and sixty five days, too many, in the year to come.

III

"What can I say to you?" I said to her.

"Tell me what's in your buckets."

"I'll tell you what's in my heart," I said. I saw her hand flash to the plastic pocket on her hip, a wooden handle, a yellow flag. "Wait!" I cried. My hand fell against my beating breast. "I have motor oil."

"Everyone has motor oil," she said. "What else?"

"Dreams," I said. "I have a recurrent dream about a clearing on a hillside." Out came the flag, but I persisted. "It's you I see coming toward me, some sunlight, not too much, your plastic suit crinkling."

She waved her flag. She took out a whistle and blew it. I opened my car door. "Don't get out of your car," she screamed. Men in mylex charged at me from all directions. Strong and wiry men with faces like swiss cheese. Toxified men with unusual attributes, too many for me to list, but, for example, horns, wings, tails, extra nipples.

"Hold it!" I screamed. I had a bucket in my hand. "Take one more step and it could be your last," I said.

"That's often the case in this line of work," said a man with three rows of teeth."

"I agree," added my love. I sensed there was something between them. I didn't care for the sight of the man. Didn't like the tone he took with me. Too much of that going around.

I pointed to my bucket. A standard five-gallon white outfit with a red circle on the side and a diagonal line cutting through.

"What do you want?" asked my sweetheart. I had wanted to keep my composure. I had wanted everything to work out differently, but of course there are too many variables, always too much to take into account.

I pointed to the man with the unwinsome dentifrice. "I want to be clear," I said, shrillness leaking into my voice. "Take one more step and it WILL BE your last."

"Fine," he said, "I just didn't want any misunderstandings."

"What else do you want?" She asked. She had eyes like none I'd ever seen. A breathtaking forehead. She wore her respirator well.

"I want it all to stop," I said. "Don't you understand?"

"That's a tall order," said a man with two tongues. "Stopping starts at home."

"That's enough out of you," I said. "More than enough."

"You really shouldn't have gotten out of your car, though," my dream said to me. Her eyes were only kindness. Absorbing eyes. We might have backfloated in one of the oceans together. We might have achieved silence. I felt her rubber glove against my knuckles. My bucket passed into her hands.

"I want it all to stop. All of it."

"Want it all," she said.

"To stop," I said.

"I'm with you there," she said.

"Where? Where?" I asked. "Where?"

The Logic of the Heart

DR. LOVELL ORDERED THE TESTS—back x-rays, sonogram—and set up a schedule of PT, contingent upon the results of the x-rays and the persistence of Leo's symptoms. His chief complaint: Come on, I'm only thirty-six years old and when I stop peeing, I ought to stop. "Maybe it's my bladder sphincter," he offered.

"Maybe." Dr. Lovell said.

"But that doesn't account for the pain in my back or the numbness in my leg."

"No," she said. Leo watched the top of her pen. She was making checkmarks on a page he couldn't see, at least ten of them. She had a look around her eyes that reminded him of an old friend. The friend—he remembered fondly the sound of her laugh.

"I'm decomposing, Doctor," Leo said. "I'm melting," he said in the voice of the wicked witch.

"We'll see." Dr. Lovell suppressed a chuckle. She clicked her pen and slid it into the pocket of her labcoat. She took the pen out again and pressed its point to her lower lip.

"Maybe you're still shaky after that hernia check thing," Leo said, batting his eyes. She looked up and then made some more checks, faster than he could count.

"You're being funny, Mr. Schwartz. We'll wait and see what the tests tell us."

Three weeks passed before Leo went to Santa Rosa Community Hospital to have his tests. Some of his symptoms alleviated shortly after the visit with Dr. Lovell. Back pain and leg numbness diminished to nuisance proportions after he bought a new pair of work shoes with decent heels. He still woke with stiffness and felt some tingling in his left instep after long drives in the car, but predictable pain is manageable pain, not so anxiety producing. The nightly images of potato-shaped tumors had relented. As for the leaking, he wore his light tan trousers to work without worry. But then there were complications, new needs and old fears.

A little background: Leo has been afraid of dying for ten years. Only recently, since he was hired as full time janitor by the Sonoma County School District, did he obtain health insurance. He can see doctors now, but he's lived with fear and uncertainty so long, he doesn't know how to live without them.

Ten years ago in New York City, Leo lost his love. Her name: Bitch. Her name: I hate you. She met another man and she vanished from Leo's life. She was there and then she was gone and Leo never had the opportunity to tell her what she took with her. There seemed to be a significant reduction in colorful flatware. There had been some silky things. She took the music and dancing and kissing and touching. She left single-serving frozen meals. He won't talk about it. He can't.

And coincidentally, ten years ago, on the night of the disappearance of Bitch, he watched a woman with cancer curling and dying, curling and rising and dying, like, not like a simple loss of vitality. She was the mother of a mentally retarded man whose case Leo had been assigned to manage. She was the world to her son, but Leo barely knew her. He saw her teeth huge and the skin on her skull no thicker than grape skin and her snake-like writhing. She was in a bed with chrome sidebars and white sheets that had turned pink from bleeding in the washer. A punchline: The sight of her scared the piss out of Leo. But it wasn't her, or she wasn't her to him. She was inhabited. In the room there was the shell of her, there was Leo and there was something else, a new acquaintance.

"Hello Leo. Pick up the phone."

Pam, the radiologist at Community, was tight-lipped about Leo's test results. If he wanted to know anything, he'd need to speak to the doctor at his local clinic. All right, he thought, this will be embarrassing. Dr. Lovell will wonder why I waited so long to have my tests. Sonograms are expensive, as Pam had sourly informed him. All right, he thought, all right, at least I know Dr. Lovell likes me. He called the Guerneville Neighborhood Health Center. May I speak to Dr. Lovell? She's no longer there? My case has been given to whom? Will you spell that for me? You've got to be kidding.

Leo calls work at 6:30 am to tell the machine that he won't be in. Now Leo's picking at a piece of electrical tape that bandages a crack in his dashboard. Now he's walking up a wooden ramp to the GNHC. A wheelchair as wide as the ramp is descending—a man who seems to have been misassembled, his chin planted on his shoulder as his eyes strain to the path in front. Leo backs down. He takes the stairs. He's glad he wore his dark trousers.

"Would you please have a seat," says the receptionist. He taps a hollow tune on his computer keyboard. "Dr. Payne will be with you in a minute."

Say it's mid-autumn, you are walking down a country road, full of the fullness. The quivering petals of a hydrangea bush, a eucalyptus is stripping off its bark for you, the smell of dirt and grass and wind. A goldfinch, a red-winged black bird, you're on your way to coffee. Someone you love is waiting. You want to hurry but you won't. You're swelling. Clover and mustard, a long white post and rail fence at your side. Someone has stapled chicken-wire to the fence, as high as the bottom of the top rail, about five feet. You are shaken by an explosion of dog, shrill, enraged, bounding toward you on the opposite side of the fence. Your hair, well it's kind of a metaphor, is not exactly standing; but its hair is all the way up, teeth all the way out and there's no one, and what you fear most, now that you can attach a what to that paralyzing sensation, is a gap in the fence, and yes, only fifteen feet away. Don't let it see that you're afraid. But it's a dog, it smells fear. It's on the road in front of you, front legs splayed, head low, hair and teeth. You can't walk around it. You think you oughtn't stop. You try to recover that full feeling, that inner glow thing. You're uniquely conscious of your buttocks, your groin, the soft white flesh beneath your chin, you're very close. You extend a hand, palm downward because someone once told you that is the right thing to do. You didn't tell your legs to stop, they just stopped. Your hand is out in space. The dog is lowering, gathering.

"The doctor can see you now, Mr. Schwartz," says the receptionist. The door is open and Leo sees a white sleeve. He walks toward Dr. Payne. The two men are equal in height, but the doctor stands taller. His hair is obsidian and full. Leo's looks like an old Brillo pad. Leo extends his hand and catches a swish of air from the back of the doctor's labcoat, an antiseptic smell. He follows down a short hall and enters the room Dr. Payne indicates with a flat hand.

"You're mad at me," Leo says, a little petulant. He believes that if doctors, cops, muggers, and the clerks at the Department of Motor Vehicles get to know him personally, are given some reason to think about who he is, then they are more likely to treat him with compassion. His belief has not been confirmed by his experience—in fact, more often lately his method has produced the most undesirable results—but the alternative, believing that who he is is of no consequence to these bearers of his fate, that he is just a part of the faceless mass of suffering humanity, well, that he can't tolerate.

"I've never met you Mr. Schwartz. Please sit down."

"On the chair?"

"On the table."

"Of course. You're going to examine me."

"Would you breathe for me?" He puts his stethoscope an inch beneath Leo's left shoulder blade.

"I'm breathing for you?" Leo says. "Which one of us is sick?"

"Breathe in, please."

He runs through the usual battery—looks in Leo's ear, hits him on the knee, pushes down on his foot. Leo makes a few more undignified attempts at humor, but it's useless. Dr. Payne is an automaton. Competence is irrelevant.

"Have you ever heard of somatization?" the doctor says.

"Like psychosomatic? Like it's all in my head?"

"Your symptoms may be real," he says.

"There's no may be," Leo says, "my jockeys are moist."

"But the cause of those symptoms may begin in your head."

"I'm almost speechless," Leo says. "Is that what you learned by looking in my ear and hitting me on the knee with that thing? I wanted to like you, Dr. Payne, but I had a feeling even before—"

"The point is," the doctor says in the most perfunctory tone, "your tests all came up negative."

"More tests then," Leo says.

"I'm going to make you a referral," Dr. Payne says. "Dr. Rott."

"Say that name again."

"R-o-t-t. He's a psychiatrist."

"I don't understand. I only know I can't go through this again. Why won't you answer?"

Leo suffered more symptoms: inflammation and bleeding of the gums, rapid hair loss, spots on his left iris, dizziness, diarrhea. He seemed to be constantly sweating, but retaining fluids. He had a pain in his chest. You're wondering about Ms. Bitch. Ms. I Hate You. But that's not the story Leo's telling. After her, he swore off relationships. He met women, sure. He had sex now and again, but no commitments. None of that *what do you really think of my poetry?* and certainly not *what color should we paint the living room?* What Leo wants is here. What he wants is now. Or he doesn't want it. And he doesn't want to talk about it.

Name: Leonard Schwartz
Occupation: Maintenance, El Molino Junior High School
Married: No
Spouse's occupation: N/A
Number to call in case of emergency: N/A
Medications: Relaxation tea.
Phobias: Dogs, cancer, the future.
Depression: Once. I thought it would never end.
Anxiety: Are you kidding?
Appetite: I eat when I'm hungry. I haven't been hungry for a while.
Sexual function: See above.
Sleep: No. I'm on leave from my job. Time is running out. I don't know how I'm going to pay for this if I lose my benefits.

The woman behind the semicircular desk had been laughing into the receiver of her phone. She cupped her hand over the mouthpiece to tell Leo, "Dr. Rott can see you in a minute." Now she is laughing again.

The doctor comes out of his office and crosses the carpeted waiting room with his hand extended. He resembles the principal at El Molino, a man Leo happens to like. He likes the doctor's khaki pants and flannel shirt, the bushy hair on his forearms, the soft easy smile. He likes the way he narrows his eyes, seems to want to read Leo's lips, seems to want to take in all of him; but Leo was not prepared to like him. Who can you trust?

"Hello Leo," he says.

"Hello Dr. Rott."

"You can call me Frank."

"And you can call me Mr. Schwartz," Leo tells him. Dr. Rott laughs and then his face displays a dozen rapid permutations, including a questioning glance at the receptionist.

"Well, have a seat, Mr. Schwartz," he says. He closes his door behind Leo and walks around to the recliner behind his desk.

"Tell me exactly why you've come," he says. His elbows are on his desk and his hands support his large head. His expression is vaguely friendly, could change in an instant.

"What did Dr. Payne tell you about me?" Leo says.

"Not much, really. Customarily—"

"He's not very personable."

"Was that your impression?"

"Did he tell you I wet myself?"

"Yes."

"And about my back pain?"

"Yes, but not in detail."

"Did he tell you it's all in my head?"

"No. Not exactly." Dr. Rott sits back and appears to examine his cuticles. Now he's interested in the fabric on the arm of his chair.

"Well, what did he say, Doctor?"

"I wonder if you would allow me to ask you a few questions?" Before Leo heard the noise that became the dog that paralyzed him, he heard silence.

"I'm sure the two of you had a good laugh." Leo's voice sounds hollow in his head. When he looks out the window it's as if he's looking through the wrong side of a telescope—the world falling away.

"Tell me why you failed to fill in the second page of my questionnaire?" The doctor leans forward.

"It seemed irrelevant."

"Tell me about your education." Dr. Rott appears to be perched on the edge of his desk.

"My education?"

"Yes. The second page of my questionnaire." There's no ambiguity on the doctor's face.

"That's going to help us understand why I carry extra briefs in my briefcase? That's not why I'm here." Leo's louder, more shrill than he means to be. Doctor Rott's not shaken, nor any less determined.

"I'm not sure why you're here, Mr. Schwartz. Maybe you don't feel this is a good use of your time." And outside his door would be a laughing secretary, and beyond her, a carpet, two left turns, an elevator and such quiet.

"I went to NYU."

He waits.

"I studied social work. I didn't finish. I completed all of my course work, but needed more hours of internship for my degree."

He waits. Leo remembers having had this talk with his parents ten years ago.

"I couldn't do it any more, Doctor. It just wasn't for me."

"Something happened?"

"Plenty happened. I can't talk about it."

"You can't talk about it?"

"I'm sorry, Doctor, was I mumbling?"

"Are you happy with your career?"

"Career?"

"At the high school. You're a janitor."

"You think I'm an under-achiever. You don't know how many times I've heard that."

"Really. What do you think?"

"I don't like to go into a filthy bathroom. Do you?"

"What about relationships, Mr. Schwartz?"

"You know, Doctor, I guess I have to trust you know what you're doing, but it sure seems—"

"Trust helps."

"Because I don't know where any of this is leading or what it's got to do with—"

"You live alone?"

"What did Dr. Payne say to you? What exactly?"

"He said you behaved very strangely at the clinic."

"What strangely?"

"He said he thought you were trying your hardest to get a rise out of him."

"A pulse would be more like it."

"He said you put cotton swabs in your ears and nose."

"A joke."

"That's quite a joke."

"I guess I was a little edgy."

"A little." Dr. Rott stands and stretches. He takes a deep breath and he leans into his desk like a big cat. "I don't know you very well, Mr. Schwartz. I believe you were anxious."

"Do you?" Leo's eyes study a tuft in the carpet. It looks like a mouse.

"Maybe dying scares you. It scares me. Maybe living—"

"Well," Leo stands, reflexively he folds his hands in front of his crotch, "I feel this has been very productive and I'm sorry, but I have other obligations."

"Right now?" says Dr. Rott. "I see." He makes eleven faces as he leads Leo to the door, one of them a smile. "If you decide you'd like to come back, please call Claudia," he nods to his laughing receptionist, "and make an appointment."

Leo had been coping. The books, the tapes, the relaxation tea, daily hikes in the redwood park, he had been healing. The very fact that he went to see Dr. Lovell was an enormous step. Wearing well-heeled shoes helped for a while.

An unsolicited diagnosis from his friend, Ed, the principal at El Molino: "Sometimes you're a real asshole, Leo." And a prescription: "Why don't you just call her, for chrissakes. Say you're sorry."

"Her" is Kris, once the librarian at the high school, a temp worker filling in for the sour-faced Ms. Filbert who had gone out with an appendicitis. Kris is the sufficient cause of all Leo's symptoms. She has plum-colored hair that falls evenly from the top of her head and curls beneath her ears and she wears reading glasses on a rhinestone chain and she's from a· tiny village in eastern Europe that Leo's never heard of and she has the kind of explosive laugh people develop when they spend hours in places where they must be quiet and she has a three-year-old daughter and ten thousand miles away a husband who is probably never coming back. Once, after school hours, she took Leo's floor buffer into the hall, turned it on high and performed a beautiful and bizarre waltz until he had to rescue her and the buffer from spinning over the top of the stairwell. Once, she put her hand on his on top of the card catalogue. Once, they kissed in the periodicals. Once, he blindly plucked a murder mystery from the standing rack beside her desk and she refused to let him check it out. She gave him *The Collected Poems of Dylan Thomas* and a handsome picture book about herbs in Northern California. "There are many kinds of mystery," she said. And he said, "I guess you're one." And once, after they'd made love, Kris fell asleep and Leo meditated on the pale curve of her hip. His moonlight. He thought, what if I can't live without you? It was Kris whom he was to meet for coffee when he was seized by his worst paralyzing panic attack.

Afterward he'd received a succession of messages on his answering machine from Kris:

"Leo, what happens? I wait over an hour. I get babysitter. Are you OK?"

And, "Leo, where do you go? Nobody seems to know? Are you OK? Call me."

And, "Leo, call me. Something not good. I've got news. I must must talk to you"

And finally, "I'm going, Leo. Speaking to your dumb stupid machine, I can't believe. I can have job on the East Coast, but if you just call, you know, if you, I don't know, Leo, I thought you want to be with me. Hello, Leo. Leo. Good bye, Leo."

The line is busy. Leo counts to ten. He presses redial. Busy. Busy. "Is this Claudia? What is this, your own private chat line? Never mind who this is." He slams down the receiver and runs to the bathroom to examine something he'd coughed into the toilet an hour ago. Is there a fleck of blood in it? Busy. Redial. Busy. Redial.

"Dr. Rott's office."

"This is Mr. Schwartz. I need to see the doctor. Put me on hold? Wait. No, wait." She doesn't wait. There is no music on hold, just a hollow sound. Leo feels panic coming on, an image of snarling dogs tearing at his throat. Breathe in. Breathe out. "No, I didn't call before. I don't think I like what you're suggesting." In. Out.

"The doctor may have an open slot on Wednesday the twenty fourth," she says.

"That's three weeks away!"

"Please hold."

"Don't put me on hold again," he manages, before he releases the phone and drops to his knees clutching his chest, before he almost passes out. But he can't pass out. Passing out would be a blessing.

"How about the sixteenth Mr Schwartz? Hello? Hello?"

The wind blows a laurel leaf against his window pane. Something sad and beautiful the way the tallest trees bend. A shirt on a laundry line inflates and then folds in upon itself. The silence of windows, and now the faint sound of a car door closing, a dog barking, the silence of hearing and not seeing, the silence of touching glass, the silence of hiding. Leo is beyond exhaustion, defenseless. He feels a rush like wind on his heart. Fear and desire: laurel leaves blowing by. Most of an hour has passed and Leo hasn't moved his head from the carpet. He's never looked at his living room from this position. The ceiling is a perfect white rectangle. He thinks, a man named Leo lives here. And if he is not careful, he will die here. The phone rings.

He picks up the receiver and says, "Please never put me on hold."

"Hello," he says. "Hello?" He screams, "Who is this? Speak! Please!"

He breathes deep. "I'm sorry," he says, "I'm so sorry. I've been expecting you."

Transactional Paralysis

"I'm not OK, You're OK / I'm not OK, You're not OK
I'm OK, You're not OK / I'm OK, You're OK."
                                    —Thomas Anthony Harris

"Simple transactional analysis is concerned with diagnosing
which ego state implemented the transactional stimulus,
and which one executed the transactional response."
                                    —Eric Berne, M.D.

"At the height of being in love the boundary between ego
and object threatens to melt away."
                                    —Sigmund Freud

CHAPTER 1
The Beginning Of The End

My wife, Jackie, spreads jelly on toast and puts it in a plastic
pouch. She makes the familiar scramble for car keys, handbag and
beeper, then comes to the kitchen table where I sit with coffee.
Mornings are hard for us. We tend to be preoccupied. Either she's
off to the hospital to play nurse or I'm off to school to play teacher.
Evenings are not much better. Cold, clipped communication.

"Well, I got to go," she says, "but there's something I should
tell you."

"Feed her something green," I say through a yawn.

"Yes, of course, but something else."

"Don't forget the sunblock."

She pinches her upper lip. She pinches her lower lip.

"What already?"

"I'm your mother, Ed. I am." She exhales. "There, I said it."

"You mean all that stuff we talked about," I say, "cotton nightgowns with floral prints, the way you like to brush my hair, that stuff?"

"No, that's not what I mean." She gives me a very quick kiss on the cheek and leaps to the doorway. "I mean I'm your mother. I never wanted." She's gone. The object of her verb, gone with her.

I search the counter top for something sharp. I find a two-pronged fork. This will make quick work. One shot for two eyes, never again to see the light of day, the faces of my loved ones. It's a substantial fork, too. I've seen Jackie turn a twenty-five pound turkey with it. Never to see that again, either. I hold the fork an inch from my nose and ponder what I might never see again. One. Two. Three. Curses! My imagination and my resolve are anemic.

CHAPTER 2

Ego States: Parent-Adult-Child

The Goob, as we call our three-year-old, has shown recent impulses of maturity. She comes padding into the kitchen from her bedroom with one finger twisted in her hair. "Here's my pacifier, Daddy. Would you hold it for me please?" I watch her plant her feet and pull the refrigerator door open. It takes a lip-biting moment but she doesn't whine or even ask for help. She finds the can of sliced beef with gravy and carries it to the cat dish. Feeding the cats is her only job. At first it gave her a great thrill and she wiggled her hips when we praised her for it. Now she proceeds with the equanimity of Charles Bronson, hit man.

"What will it be, Goob, Cheerios or a waffle?"

"I don't think I'm hungry."

"Oh, well maybe after you get your clothes on."

"Maybe," she says. "Maybe I could wear my princess dress."

"Yes," I say, "of course you can, sweetie."

"And we could play princesses."

"Princesses?"

"And you could be a princess, too. You could wear Mommy's dress."

I'm happy to hear the rise in her pitch, don't like to think of her as prematurely sober, but "I don't know, honey," I say. "It seems like there's too much else going on."

"Then you could be the prince." She's not at all deflated.

"That might be all right. What do I do?"

"You have to kiss me."

"Oh."

"On the mouth."

"Oh."

She approaches me with the slightest sashay in her boyish little hips, an odd mistiness in her eyes. She holds my head in her hands, little thumbs and fingers pinching the hair of my sideburns. She doesn't know how to pucker. It's a slobbery event.

I stand up quickly. "OK," I say, "now we kissed. Now what?"

"Do it again," she says.

"Well, I don't know. What about another game? What if we read *Rabbit Rabbit*?" She looks adult hurt, like her mother, my mother, looks sometimes. "Maybe you're too old for that one. What about *The Big Book of Tell Me Why*?"

She walks to her bedroom and closes the door. I feel guilty, that I've betrayed her, but I resist the temptation to kneel at her bedside and beg forgiveness. I stare at the two-pronged fork.

Perhaps, I think, I need more information. The phone rings fatefully.

CHAPTER 3

More Information

"Hello," I say.

"Hi Ed." It's the woman I have taken to be my mother for as

long as I can remember. She might be the best impostor there ever was. "I'm a little surprised to catch you at home."

"Oh," I say. "And what does that mean?"

"I thought that on a beautiful morning such as it is, you and The Goob would already be out to the playground."

"You called, nonetheless." This woman and I haven't been close since I married Jackie. I take it that she's jealous and I'm told that such feelings are not uncommon for widowed mothers whose only sons are married. But what about my feelings?

"Is something wrong, Ed?"

"It's not something I think I can talk to you about."

"Something between you and Jackie?"

"Have you been talking to Jackie, Mom?"

"I've been wanting to talk to her. I kind of wanted to thank her for the baby pictures. But there's something else. Actually, I think I should talk to you first."

"There's no time like the present—right, Mom?"

"It's not easy for me to bring this up, Ed."

"I'd imagine it's not, Mom."

"Maybe it should wait. You seem to be—"

"Maybe it shouldn't wait." Now it feels as if the dining room floor is tilting toward the kitchen, the kitchen leaning against the two-pronged fork. "Maybe it's time to come clean," I say.

"I was looking at the pictures," she says.

"Mom."

"I was studying them."

"Yes."

"I don't think The Goob looks like Jackie."

"Of course she does."

"No," she says. "Not at all."

"I sure don't understand what you're talking about."

"Were you there," says the woman I have believed to be my mother for as long as I've believed anything, "when The Goob was born?"

"You know I was."

"Were you in the room?"

"I was." I feel dizzy, hear unearthly shrieks, like from a sixties horror film. "I was, right up until...you know."

"You passed out."

"What are you trying to say?"

"I don't know, Ed. I wish I had an explanation."

I sit. Stand. Sit. "I'm almost speechless," I say. It's the last thing I say.

"I'm going to let you go now," she says. "I think I hear Roger calling."

CHAPTER 4
Junior College

I swallow hard and dial Mom.

"Hello," she says.

"Who's Roger?"

"Oh Blessed God In Heaven," she says. "I can't believe I forgot to mention."

"Who is he, Mom?"

"Well, I'm not sure where to start. I met him at the senior center. He's a volunteer. It was, you know, Wednesday, Bag Day, and you know, I always overfill my bags. They had a surplus of Rice-A-Roni, which is small in those little boxes, but surprisingly heavy. And of course the canned goods."

"But..."

"He's the sweetest young man. You're really going to like him. And he has these shoulders that couldn't have been sculpted so round, so perfect."

"He helps you sometimes."

"You might know him, Ed. He takes classes at the Junior College. He's interested in history. He might be in one of your classes. He often wears a Metallica T-shirt with the sleeves cut-off."

"And he helps you around the house with this and that."

"This and that," my mother giggles. "He wants me to marry him, honey."

"You forgot to mention!"

"Listen, don't be upset. He's a little bit nervous about you."

"I bet, but MOM!"

"I was wondering if you could do me one favor."

"MOM!"

"I was wondering if it would be OK with you, you know, if you could call him Dad."

CHAPTER 5

A Not Very Useful Talk With My Unconscious

Ed: Hey, my life was going along fine. I was happy in my job, in love with my family, reasonably healthy, you know, a little money put away finally, etc. Tell me, why is this shit coming up right now?

Unconscious: Tell me, do you really want to know? Because my advice is, drop it.

Ed: Today I find out that I may be married to my mother. My wife may not be the real mother of my daughter. My new dad is ten years younger than I am and a student in my class. And I think I have a little bit of a crush on The Goob.

Unconscious: Sure, but are you happy?

Ed: I'm going out of my mind. We are.

Unconscious: You didn't answer my question.

Ed: Who's calling the shots, anyway?

Unconscious: Hmmm.

Ed: Because look at history. People hurt themselves over this kind of thing. And of course there's the other side to consider, the floods, droughts, and pestilence. If this is what I think it is, it's not just me that's cursed. I have responsibilities, don't I?

Unconscious: And let's say that we don't look at history, you know, as a kind of a thought experiment. You forget and I, you know, misfile. It will be our secret.

Ed: Then we're lost!

Unconscious: OK then, we're lost.

Ed: I'm not OK with that. I'm not OK and you're not OK.

Unconscious: But I feel fine, really.

CHAPTER 6

Investigation

"Come on, Goob," I say. "We're going to the supermarket. I've got to find out what the hell's going on in the world." I open her bedroom door and find her with her head stuck in the sleeve of her pink princess dress, the one with the tutu attached. "We can get a treat," I say.

"We'll see," she says. We make the adjustments painlessly. We manage to get the sandals on and buckled without any of the usual complications.

We're driving past the bend in the road where the river is visible through a gap in the trees. It appears to be neither high nor low, nor is it blood red, nor do I see cattle or the carcasses of neighbors' pets floating by. "Maybe I could go for a popsicle," says The Goob.

"That's the spirit," I say.

"But it seems a little early in the day for that kind of a treat," she says.

I happen to have survived a couple of small "d" natural disasters in this town. In the summer it's a pleasant vacation community, but in winter the glistening river swells into a muddy brown behemoth and the wind whips frenzy into the crowns of the kingly bays and oaks. What's a disaster look like?

Stage 1: You can't find parking within two hundred yards of the Safeway.

Stage 2: If you're not up to the minute, you can forget about finding the survival essentials: batteries, bottled water, candles, peanut butter. You can't even purchase a deck of cards. What you find are wet footprints by the frozen foods section and specials on smarmy sliced turkey breast. You see signs of big and small panic. People forgetting to log their expenditures in their checkbooks. Mothers pressing their small children's heads hard into their kneecaps. Sometimes you see evidence of true heroism. I saw a man offer his suspenders to a woman so that she could fasten down the top of her broken convertible sportscar. If she'd had to drive with the top down, her children would have gotten wet and probably caught some nasty colds. She thanked him and offered a few dollars, which he did not accept. He gave her a soul handshake and said something which made me think of Tom Joad. Five minutes later I saw the same man pushing a cart full of empty cans and bottles with one hand, the other held the front of his trousers in a fist.

Stage 3: You get home. You stare at the black face of the television. You light a candle. You gather odd things around you and call them precious. You feel silly counting cigarettes, aspirin and chocolate bars. Your looks are furtive. There's an awful silence before the timeless elements arrive and beat down upon the accouterments of your modern-day existence.

I take The Goob out of her carseat and sling her up onto my shoulders. There is perhaps a slightly greater number of cars in the lot than one would expect midway between the lunch and dinner rush. One man has a bag of charcoal briquets on the bottom rung of his shopping cart. Not a panic purchase. One woman is leaning against the back door of her pick-up. Her tone of voice, the wrinkle between her eyes suggest that she's offering an involved explanation. I hear the words "inner child" and "exercise bike." There's my friend Micky Einstein. He listens to the radio station that plays all news and he listens almost all of the time. "What's up Micky?" I say.

"I had the strangest dream," he says.

He reaches up and tweaks The Goob's earlobe and she says, "Do you still like treats?"

"I love them," he says.

"What about the dream?" I ask.

"I was in the Norwegian Bicycle Army."

"Oh?"

"And we were raping and pillaging a small town in the north of Holland."

"Really?"

"I got off my bike and chased down a woman in a coat made of rat fur."

"Hey, that's pretty weird," I say.

"The woman was Hillary Clinton."

"Oh wow. Then what happened?"

"We found a little foxhole and shared a can of sardines and the last sips of a bottle of wheat beer."

"That's it?"

"What do you want?" He seems a little offended.

"It's just that it all seemed a little apocalyptic, you know."

"Maybe," he says. "It was great. She was really nice."

"Huh," I say. "Well maybe we could talk sometime. I'm actually in kind of a hurry right now."

When we pass through the automatic glass doors, The Goob twists and I bend and she lowers herself down from my shoulders, two tight fists in my flannel shirt. I turn her shoulders and point her to the popsicle section. I find a stack of *Examiners* where they should be, beside the rack of sour-dough bread.

Headlines: *HISTORIC UFW-GALLO CONTRACT, COLLEGE TUITIONS OUT OF REACH FOR MOST AMERICANS, REPUBLICANS BLOCK TEST BAN TREATY.* What bullshit, I mumble. But it's not extraordinary bullshit, I think. *GAS, THE NEW WAY TO BAR-B-Q.* I wonder what the alternative presses have to say, but I won't find one in Safeway.

Finally, and with some trepidation, I move to the tabloids at the checkstand, the real heart of my investigation.

There's Slim Shady again, marital trouble. There's Oprah, looking fit. There's Brad, Bruce, Jennifer, Demi. New handsome photos of JFK, Jr. There's a black and white picture of a cloud. I hold it up in such a way so that light can penetrate the gloss on the page. I see Sinatra's profile, a cocktail in his hand. *OLE BLUE EYES TRAPPED IN GRAY SKIES, WIFE SWALLOWS HUBBIE'S VIAGRA—INSTANTLY PREGNANT, 500 POUND MAN FINDS WEIGHT HE LOST.*

The Goob waddles up to the checkstand, a box of twenty-four assorted popsicles in her hands.

"How did you get that?"

"I like this kind," says a grandmotherly woman behind her, pointing to a picture of a red rocket pop. The Goob shrugs.

"Is that what you wanted, Sweetie?"

"It's OK, Daddy," says The Goob. "It will be OK."

"Because if it's not," I begin, and I see a hint of strain in her big soft cheeks, and then, I see on page three of *The Star*, what I think I've been looking for.

CHAPTER 7
WOMAN GIVES BIRTH TO ADULT MAN—MARRIES HIM!

Let me try to summarize: A team of obstetricians who'd come out from behind the iron curtain some years ago disappeared into a north coast California cult. One of the esteemed doctors had been experimenting with fertility drugs. Another was studying the effects of Human Growth Hormone when administered at various stages in the development of a fetus. Yet another was on the cutting edge of cloning technologies. Beneath a block of text is a series of photos and captions which describe the ordinary passage of an egg from the ovaries to the uterine wall. There is nothing remarkable about the first three pictures if you are at all familiar with the mystery of life, but in the fourth the egg is lifted out of the diagram and blown up many thousands of times, such that one can see a fully grown man, and believe it, fully dressed, curled like a fetus. Subsequent photos show a woman in bridal attire, a white veil covering her face, arm in arm with a smiling but waxy-looking groom. The last paragraph of the article explains that many women who've lost their husbands to extraterrestrials cannot bear the idea of starting over with someone else. With the help of Russian scientists and the latest cloning technologies, some of these women have given birth to their own spouses.

I'm thinking what you're thinking, right? How can you clone someone who's been abducted?

Page four of *The Star*: MAN CLONED FROM FINGER-PRINTS!

CHAPTER 8
I Can Hide From The Truth As Well As Anyone

But, I can't seem to let go of a good riddle. Jackie, on the other hand, is easily stumped by the *Daily Word* Jumble in the paper. "How do you do it?" She's asked me.

"It's easy," I always tell her. "Relax. Just don't focus. Let your attention drift."

The Goob presses STOP on the VCR. No more *Bananas In Pajamas*. The remote looks enormous in her hand, but she knows what to do. She flicks through programs until she comes to pause on a PBS special about the aftermath of Desert Storm. We see decimated buildings, children with slings and red bandages, cracks and craters in the dry earth. We see black smoke and black water. The voice-over is a hoarse whisper, then it goes silent. The camera closes in on a gosling soaked in oil. "That's not real, is it?" asks The Goob.

"It can't be," I say.

"It's too yucky," she decides and flicks to something else.

I put three lengths of turkey kielbasa in a sizzling pan, three potatoes in the microwave. Jackie will be home soon and I don't know what to say to her. I need to speak with someone. My friend Einstein would not be much help to me now. When I've been depressed, I've enjoyed his company. To him life is a ride at the amusement park. He has his downs as well as his ups, but he never questions the rusty and rickety scaffold underneath. Sure, he's eating sardines in a bunker with The First Lady. Why not?

What I need is penetrating analysis. What I need is a context for my experience. I need moral and intellectual support and now. I dial Dr. Fitzmore. Students have told me he's very intense—a bastard, in fact. He teaches Introduction To The Classics. He's been at The Junior College for twenty-five years and the rumor is that he's never given an A.

"Hello," he says.

"Hi Dr. Fitzmore, this is Ed from History."

"Do I know you?" I hear odd music in the background. I figure it's ancient music.

"We met once at a faculty thing," I say. I hear something like wailing, something like moaning. "But I wouldn't expect you to remember me."

"I have an excellent memory."

"Yes, but there's no reason." There's a weighty pause. "I asked you if you were familiar with a cheese on a plate."

"It was Gorgonzola. You're rather tall."

"Yes."

"OK, please continue."

"Well," I say, "I have this friend."

"Oh?"

"My friend is married." I don't know why I'm mumbling. I hear screams of pain.

"So, you have a married friend?" he says. He shouts, "Hold still!" And then to me, "Please, go on."

"This friend is married. This friend is married to his. I can't say it."

"Wait just a minute," he says. "Back up!" He shouts. "Hold it there. Hold it!"

"I'm married to my wife, Dr. Fitzmore," I say.

"Good for you," he says. "Have I met her?"

"My wife is my mother!"

"Hold it!" He shouts. "We'll have to continue this later."

"Excuse me," I say.

"That's very unusual, Ed," he says. "What about your father?"

"I never met my real father. I mean, I don't think I have. I'm told he died before I was born."

"Hmmm." Another long pause. "How's everything going?" Dr. Fitzmore asks.

"Not bad, I guess."

"Have you ever slain anyone? Think hard."

"No."

"Good. I think that's good."

"And have you consummated this marriage with your mother?"

"Sure. Plenty."

"Children?"

"One girl." I hear footsteps, the knob turning. It's Jackie. "But I'm not sure she's mine. Or hers. My wife's. My mother's." It's a cordless phone. I'm whispering as I pass through the French glass doors from the kitchen onto the deck. "What can you tell me, Dr. Fitzmore?"

"Some people say the world has changed," he says. "Look at education standards. When I was a schoolboy I studied Latin and Greek. I read The Classics. I had a sense of history and I thought I understood my place. My place, you know?"

"Please Doctor quickly." Jackie is tickling The Goob on the bed. When the squealing subsides, she'll come looking for me.

"I think you're in for hell," he says. "Maybe some insights will come from this, but not without a great deal of suffering."

"What should I do?"

"Suffer."

"That's it?"

"As I see it, you don't have any choice."

"I'd hoped—"

"I hope you'll keep in touch. I'm very interested, you know."

CHAPTER 9

Last Chance For A Complementary Transaction (see Happiness)

"Ed, honey, I'm home."

"Oh hey," I say. I put the phone down. I dodge the kiss because under the circumstances it doesn't feel right. "How'd it go? Let me get you a beer. Sit." Jackie's expression is a mix of bewilderment and suspicion. Usually these days I'm eager to get to my work as soon as she gets home. It's been one of many sources of tension between us. We can't just talk talk because every little border skirmish turns global, every ounce of info becomes a pound of ammunition. We fight over nothing less than time and space, and there will never be enough. We're a married couple.

She sits and slowly lets her shoulders settle. I return with a cold can of Mickey's. Now she looks simply exhausted. "You don't want to hear about my day," she says. "Just woe and misery."

"Really?" The frying pan is smoking black. I run to the kitchen and run back.

"There seems to be something going around," she says, "but the symptoms are vague."

"Like?"

"You know, abdominal pain, chest pain, congestion, diarrhea, a little bit of everything. And I don't like to prescribe antibiotics unless I know."

"Some new kind of flu or something?"

"Some kind of plague," she says. And then, as if bored with our discussion, "Come here, Goob, sit on my lap. Do you want a sip of my beer?"

"You don't really mean plague?" I say.

"Tell me about your day," she says. "What'd you guys do?"

"It was a usual day," says The Goob.

"You don't really mean plague?" I say. I'm trying not to focus, trying to let my attention drift. But I feel as if I've been gutted, hollowed. I want to drop to my knees and weep. "What do you think my day was like?" I say under my breath. It didn't used to be like this. A fellow teacher told me, "Wait until the romance wears off." He's partially employed and most of his pay goes to child support, the remainder supports his taste for Winner's Cup vodka in the plastic half gallon bottle. That man is bitter. When I see him in the halls of the Junior College I turn and run, as if I've forgotten something in my office.

Before the self-help books and sex books and counseling and the countless other contrivances, Jackie would return from work and I'd hide in the closet. I'd dress in plaids, stripes, fishing boots and felt bonnet, whatever I could get my hands on, and when she opened the door I'd pounce on her. She'd scream. She'd laugh. Within a minute I'd have her out of her lab coat and cotton undies. We were playmates, wrestlers.

I'd reach the base of the stairs, dreary with my backpack full of books and papers and see Jackie at the top in her satin nightgown with a champagne glass in her hand and a finger pressed to her lips. "Ssshhh," she'd say. "I just got the baby down." She'd lead me into bed by my fingertips. We were lovers. We kept our eyes open.

We enjoyed skinnydipping and mushroom tea and poetry and soulsearching because it wasn't all play—shoveling, sanding, wallpapering—but wonder, ironically; we had a sense of wonder that enabled us to be who we could be, should be, together. We kept our promises.

"What you said this morning," I say, "do you think it's true?" She's looking down and brushing back The Goob's soft yellow curls with her fingertips. When she looks up her eyes are thick and spilling.

"Seems all we do anymore is argue," she says.

"I know."

"And it's so damn important to be right instead of—"

"Instead of what?" My hand keeps looking for something. My chest.

"You're there, but you're not there. You're not paying attention."

"I feel the same."

"Well, someone's got to take charge," she says. "Didn't we say this wouldn't happen to us?"

"We did."

"But it happened." She reaches down and turns off the television. I reach for something to fill the something.

"What are we going to do?"

"I don't know what to do," she says.

"You really think you're my mother?"

"Does it matter, Ed? Does it make any difference?"

"I need to go out for a while," I say. "I need to clear my mind, try to get a new perspective."

"What's new about that?"

"I don't know if I can live with this, Jackie."

"But you can," she says. Her eyes are dry now like the stones at the top of a beach. "Whatever you, we, might have once believed, we can live with this. That's the worst part, isn't it?"

CHAPTER 10
I'm OK—I'm Not OK

I used to ask my students on the first and last days of a semester to answer a single question in a written paragraph. The question: Why study history? The answer I got, almost invariably at the beginning and the end of the semester: Because "History repeats itself." I don't ask it anymore. History may or may not repeat itself, depending upon how one chooses to define terms. In some important sense, history is one of few disciplines which never truly repeats itself. Through the lens of an ever-changing present we interpret the past, and through an ever-changing past we experience the present. With the millennium in our rearview, we are freer than we've ever been from the past. We've reconstructed our hips, lips, noses, and finally brains, destroyed our most precious nightmares, the seeds of our oldest stories. We invent our memories in keeping with our dreams. Our dreams?

Students repeat themselves! And I've thought these thoughts many times before. It's not compelling any new insights as I wander out to the local dive. I am married to my mother. I feel heavy.

I sit on a stool and push some stray kernels of cheese popcorn across the polyurethane surface of the bar. "Give me something cold," I say to Pat. The place is packed. She looks at me with annoyance. "A draft. I don't care," I say. She sets a foamy glass of Full Sail on a coaster in front of me. I take a long sweet sip and close my eyes. It's trite but true; you hear differently with your eyes closed. I feel certain that blind people hear colors.

I hear quarters ringing into the coin slot of the pool table. The thud of fifteen balls dropping, five are rolling. Seven kinds of laughter, most of them derisive. Mock expressions of sympathy. Mock threats. Many forms of chiding. I hear many people saying the same thing: "I haven't seen you in a while." And I hear just as many saying: "Come on, what bullshit!" And these expressions are getting louder until I hear the shuffle and creak of the stool beneath me. Then very loudly and very clearly, I hear, "It's not bullshit. I was abducted!"

Of course I open my eyes, wouldn't you? But there's no one on either of the stools next to me. There's no one in the place but Pat and myself and Pat is at the far end slicing limes. I see my face in the mirror behind the bar, a boy's face. "I was abducted," it says. "Taken right out of my life, like squirted, like do you remember tiddly-winks?"

"Yes," I say.

"Or like when you push down on a watermelon seed with a dull knife."

"I get it."

"One minute I'm there, next minute I'm gone."

"Yes."

"And someone else is standing in my place."

"Me?"

"Yes. Someone with no vision, no sense of what was or what could have been."

"You're not being fair," I say. I'm loud enough to draw Pat's attention.

"Want another beer?" she says.

"Sure," I say. Then quietly, inwardly, I've had to make many adjustments. None of my roles in life are as I'd imagined them. The tweed-tenured-teacher upon whom students looked with awe and affection—that's a thing of the past. Good-bye Mr. Chips, et al. Wise-strong-father-protector. I feel that in some ways I'm the greatest threat to my little girl's well-being. In time she and her cohort will murder me and my generation for our lack of courage and vision, for having ruined the world again. Husband-provider-devoted-loving-partner-playmate. Once hiding was a game, the object was to be found.

Now I see a pitying face in the mirror. "You'll be OK," he says.

"Yes," I say. "More adjustments. New ways of not seeing. I suppose I will," I say, "but what about you?"

EPILOGUE

Everyone is OK. We are not as susceptible to the elements as people were in the past. We are sheltered from wind and rain and even shame…the blinding is not permanent, but constant.

When the multifarious natural and unnatural disasters which daily occupied the front pages briefly relented, there was space for the following headline: Summer Is Here!

Let me try to summarize briefly: Our egos and objects, our holograms, our heroes, have a family vacation because The Goob has never cooked a marshmallow on a stick. They build a campfire because that's what people do. Ed blows up an air mattress and feels a gentle wind in his head. He tosses an empty bottle of insect repellent against the doorflap of the tent. No more swatting slow mosquitoes. This is the hour of moths and bats, suggestions. In the flickers and shadows they watch each other move. Ed watches Jackie washing her hands and face in the moon-streaked pond and he's breathless. He can almost feel himself hugging her around the waist, almost feel the bridge of his nose pressed to the soft flesh of her neck. He imagines squeezing her while the earth spins out from underfoot. He watches The Goob twirl a flame-tipped stick, a red ember against the starlit sky. She is painting new constellations. Jackie pushes through tall reeds back to the fire. She sees the log upon which she will sit and every step she takes is careful, a perfection. She is humming the melody which has been a part of the bedtime routine since their daughter was born: "Twinkle Twinkle Little Star." It's the only song they all happen to know. Ed is humming the same. The Goob leads with her glowing baton, and all together, "How I wonder what you are."

Double Shift

Ruby shouts, "Don't damn you touch me!" and shoves through the screen door and onto the back porch where fellow residents puff on cigarettes around a white painted picnic table sticky from spilled coffee, smeared with ashes. Ruby abhors smoke. One of her fears is that she'll get cancer from other people's exhalations. She continues out into the yard and the flood light triggered by the motion detector catches her slapping herself on the cheeks. It's her fourth tantrum today.

Back through the screen door, through the kitchen where Gordon scrubs the plastic juice pitcher for the third time before putting it into the dishwasher, past the cubby where residents can make or receive phone calls until ten-thirty is the office, a boxy room with two desks, four tall file cabinets, a threadbare plaid sofa and a humming photocopy machine. The office is airless and tends to retain the dinner smell longer even than the kitchen. Tonight it stinks heavy like the kielbasa and steamed cabbage Carl cooked. Trish is brushing her hair and searching a desktop for a black pen to complete her charting. She'll put a note in the Comm. Log about Ruby's behavior and a recommendation for a med eval. It's a few minutes after eleven and she's waiting for relief.

Johnson, short for Mike Johnson, works as an on-call relief counselor for a large social service agency with four group homes. The Open Door serves as a sixty-day shelter for homeless folks with mental illness. The Bugel House is for teens referred by the

California Youth Authority. Burger House is for adults with mild to moderate retardation. Johnson fills in most often at the Burger House. The Path is the home for men and women with dual diagnoses—substance abuse and mental illness. Each of the homes has its own staff and management, its own rules and jargon. Johnson rarely works at The Path because it is a long drive from his home. He will take a double shift if he is called, then the drive seems worthwhile. But, Johnson dreads the double shift at The Path. He is driving not too fast down 101 toward Cotati, looking for the moon and feeling acid rise in his throat. He is about to clock in for a sixteen-hour gig.

Johnson has been with The Agency for seven years. Many times he has wanted to call the main office and tell Patricia, Vicky, Karin to erase his name from the relief list. He's angry about the seven-fifty an hour and he's bored, more than bored, sickened, depressed, by the way The Agency treats its clients, especially at The Path. The staff there are so damn self-righteous, so full of themselves. A poorly understood mission and a little authority adds up to ugly treatment. He might have taken a regular position at any one of the houses, a few years back there'd been plenty of offers, but as he tells it, I'm freer this way, I can make my own schedule. In fact, he works more hours for less pay than most full-timers. He'll tell you, "At least I don't have a boss," and in a sense it is true, but in another sense, he has many bosses and less say-so than the greenest of case managers. If pushed, Johnson will say that he's an artist, which means he's an outsider. This work is supplemental income. His real job is as a back-up singer and song-writer for an R&B band called Johnny Bourgeois and The Means of Production. Subtracting the expenses from the revenues of his show business, he has earned one hundred and ten dollars in four years.

Johnson straightens to six feet out of his Corona Hatchback. He has to lift up on the door when he closes it, reminder of a brush with a telephone pole on a wet winter night. That was the last night he'd spent with his fiancee, four years back. She'd pushed him to articulate his career choices. He'd driven home alone angry, feeling reckless. Losing grip, spinning out, it was the end of something, the beginning of something else. As he lifts up, he clutches his lower back.

"Hey Ruby," he says. He saunters to the stairs, the porch. "You OK?" Ruby moves into the shadow of a diseased Willow. "Come see me later, if you want," he says. Ruby shakes her head, a pale smile. Joy shifts her weight and he can hear her thighs unstick from the picnic bench. She squeezes out a Pall Mall and rubs her tobacco-brown fingernail with the yellow thumb and forefinger of the opposite hand.

"You're back."

"I was in the neighborhood," Johnson says. "Figured I'd stop in and earn a living."

"What a day it's been," Joy wags her head.

"A shitty day," says Javier through the screen door.

"I'll come and get the dope after pass-on," Johnson says.

"Don't say dope," Paulie giggles. Paulie's new, eighteen, the youngest of the twelve residents. He wears a goatee like Johnson, a tattoo on his wrist like Johnson, and he wants to be a musician. He rooms with Phil, which is unfortunate, but everyone says Paulie's got the stuff, the right attitude for recovery. Some of the staff hope that Paulie will be a "positive influence" on Phil.

"Sorry," Johnson says. "I mean scoop."

"Hey Gordon," Johnson says. Gordon is bent over reading the instructions on the box of dishwasher soap.

"You're late," Trish says to Johnson. "I guess it doesn't matter, I'm not finished charting yet."

"Just leave yourself a space and do it tomorrow." Johnson takes up the badly warped guitar from the rec. cabinet on his way into the office. "I'm serious. Get out of here. I heard it was a shitty day."

"It was."

"Go have a couple stiff ones."

"Funny." Trish like most of the workers at The Path is in recovery. "I want to go sit in a hot tub."

"Do it." Johnson picks blues chords, nothing fancy. "Go get soaked."

"No, I should finish up."

"Do it," Johnson sings, "get out of here, the moon is big and the night is clear."

Trish presses her cuticles hard against her lower lip. Her eyes swim across the ceiling "Quickly," she says, she screws the cap on a plastic bottle of diet cola and nestles it in her handbag, "a couple things you should know. Ruby's having intense mood swings. I think they should up her Lithium or something."

"Surprise."

"Phil's on blackout." Blackout is twenty-four hours without visitors, phone calls, television, without permission to leave the premises. Three blackouts equals expulsion—in Phil's case, a police escort to the lock-down at Atascadero.

"Surprise. What'd he do?"

"At morning check-in, you know, he never wants to say how he feels. That's all he's got to do, say how he feels and what's his goal for the day."

"Maybe his goal is *not* to say how he feels."

"Maybe, but that's rules Johnson."

"So he got blackout? You're tough."

Trish thinks. "He said, 'This is pissing me off.'"

"So what's wrong with that?"

"He said, 'My goal for today is to kick some punk ass.'"

Johnson plucks the g-string. "Seems appropriate."

"It's not. It's not appropriate." Trish lugs a pair of big black binders from the desk toward the standing file, but Johnson blocks her way. He takes the binders out of her hands.

"Go. Rest." She blows a puff of air that makes her bangs fly up, then leaves. She stops at the screen door.

"You know, it's different for you. You're not around here all the time."

"What are they paying you?" Johnson asks.

There's a pause. He doesn't expect an answer. He scans the top pages of the med file to see that everyone has received evening doses. "It'll be nine-fifty with the increase, not enough."

"What increase?"

"Oh. I guess you're not in on that. I guess it's only for full-timers."

"Fuck. You're kidding me."

"You subs'll be next, I'm sure." The door slams.

Johnson pulls a drawer from the desk and fills his palm with Tums. He says "Fuck" eleven times while he crunches, his mouth full of white paste. He puts the guitar back in the rec. cabinet and as he walks through the kitchen he says, "Wash your ears, Gordon, while you're at it." He finds an edge of bench on the picnic table and sits, straddling. He rolls a smoke. "Shitty day, eh?" He looks at Javier. "I thought you guys were heading out to Salmon Creek."

"It would've been," Joy answers, "but something with the van."

"It wasn't the van," Javier says. "It was cause of Phil." He pulls up hard on his jeans which are hanging below his butt and they fall back below his butt. "It was cause of Phil wouldn't go and they didn't have no other staff to sit here with him."

"Sounds like Phil's just settling in," Johnson says. Only the crickets respond. "It takes time," he adds.

"I didn't want to go anyway," Paulie says. "Not with this sunburn." He reveals a pink, fleshy biceps from under his sleeve.

"I wanted to go," Ruby walks up on the porch and into the house. "Get out of here and get some fresh air for a change."

The thing about Ruby, Johnson realizes as he converts the sofa in the office into a bed, is that she's kind of cute when she's not pouting. She looks like the lover from years gone by, pale as paper with henna red hair, even pouts like her. He spreads a sleeping bag across the coarse cushions, but he doesn't lie down. He takes up the guitar again:

I'm blazing through the twilight
Pleading that the sun don't set
Ruby of the red highlights
I'm not ready for the darkness yet

First staff arrives at eight A.M. Dawn. Johnson hasn't met her yet. At nine thirty, Trish. At ten, Bruce. The manager, Ted Braddock, will arrive at eleven with an over-dressed salad bar lunch in a white bag, loud greetings and hearty laughter. Ted Braddock is one of the few black men in The Agency, the only in management. He's an addict. He used to sing the blues. He's known as a no-bullshit guy and Johnson has to keep mindful of certain facts to dislike him.

Ted and Johnson first met at Sonoma State University. They took a class together called The Therapeutic Relationship and enrolled in another called The Social Work Matrix, but Braddock dropped that one in favor of Mental Health Administration. They went through The Agency's orientation together. They had a common interest, music, and what seemed like a shared suspicion for The Agency's lack of regard for clients' rights and dignity. When Braddock was promoted to management a year ago, Johnson put a note in his box: *You're smooth, buddy. I'm glad it's you. This agency needs a little soul.* And Braddock left a note for Johnson, folded, stapled in the relief box: *Time to get with the program, Mike.*

It is the responsibility of the overnight staff, Johnson in this case, to see that all residents are up, dressed and medicated by eight. Chores are done between eight and eight-thirty. Check-in is at eight-forty. The day is plotted thus with short breaks between groups, exercise, chores, and meals, lots of short breaks for bitching and smoking.

Johnson had difficulty drifting to sleep. He leafed through the charts and found nothing out of the ordinary. He took an extra minute to read Phil's psycho-social. The man was first incarcerated in 1972 at the age of twelve. He's been in and out of institutions ever since, except for a time of five years when he worked as a motorcycle mechanic in East Palo Alto. Reports to have been clean and sober during that period, until his girlfriend was killed in a crash, relapsed. When Johnson finally nodded off, he was awakened by Gordon who needed his Albuterol inhaler, a wracking hacking cough. Then there was a wrong number. Soon after came the grinding gears and wheezing hydraulics of the garbage truck just outside the window. At seven forty-five Johnson fell into a sweet dream, first swimming, then flying through shades of blue. He felt as if he were being drawn toward a bolt of light. He was startled awake by pounding at the office door.

"Morning," he wipes his eyes.

"It sure is." An officious young woman with an enormous handbag pushes through and leaves a short line of residents waiting in the doorway. "I'm Dawn," she says. "I'm new."

"Jeez, what time is it?" He holds his head low, pinching the bridge of his nose as he makes his way to the bathroom. When he returns Dawn is administering pills to Paulie. She is textbook thorough, double-checking the names and numbers on the packets against the listings in the file binder. It will take all day at this rate. "I can do this," Johnson says.

"Oh," says Dawn, "I'll go and wake up the others, I guess." She puts her big handbag under the desk. "I'm kind of excited," she says. "It's my first full shift, groups and all."

"I'm Johnson. I'm not too excited yet, but I'll see what I can do." She tilts her head, puzzled, then a sudden smile.

"Next," calls Johnson. Joy steps up with a glass of orange juice in her hand. "What'll it be, ma'am, a Serzone Screwdriver?"

"Make it a double," she laughs.

"You shouldn't joke like that," Gordon says from the doorway. He laughs.

"It's all one big joke around here," Ruby standing behind him.

"I forget," Johnson says, "you people in recovery don't have any sense of—" he stops because he sees Ruby making a white knuckle fist. "I'm sorry," he says. "I forget."

The line is five long. Others drift into the kitchen and mill around the toaster, the microwave and the two refrigerators. Dawn returns. "Well, everyone's up, except the guy in room six." She looks at a chalkboard on the wall, "Phil."

"Phil likes to sleep," Javier says. Javier has a habit of touching women in inappropriate ways. His hygiene is exceptionally poor, his pants are always falling and some of his fellow residents, particularly the women, find him repulsive. Now he leans from his position in the med line to examine Dawn's backside. Johnson's examination is more subtle. He watches and waits to see how Dawn will react. She squares up, faces Javier.

"Well, he'd better get up or he's going to get blackout," she says with stunning authority. Yep, Johnson thinks, she'll fit in.

Javier doesn't back down easily. "Phil's already on blackout," he says.

"Well, then," Dawn looks at Johnson.

"Well, then," Johnson says, "we'll have to bust a cap in his lazy ass."

Javier laughs and Dawn makes herself busy moving papers from one desk to another. She can't know what she's putting where or why, but the thump of the heavy stacks seems to satisfy some need.

"Look," Johnson says, "as soon as I finish with the meds I'll fill you in on the routine." His voice is soft, vaguely apologetic.

She pulls the orientation packet she'd been given by

Braddock out of her handbag and holds it up. "I know all about the routine," she says.

Johnson and Dawn make the rounds, check the chores. Johnson gives a perfunctory glance and a thumbs up. He doesn't like this part of his role. He doesn't like to feel that he's treating adults like children.

Dawn is a stickler, but she lavishes praise on a job well-finished. She finds dust on a bureau, a scrap of paper on the carpet, a strand of hair on the toilet seat. She gives Gordon a hug for his spotless kitchen. The performance of the residents is a reflection on her, um, professionality. Johnson feels the acid rising again. Has he contributed to this? "Look," he offers, "maybe I kid around too much. I hope you didn't feel that I was undermining you."

"You weren't undermining me," Dawn says. "I know what I'm doing. I know what these people have been through." It's apparent she's been working herself up to this. "I've been there."

"Yea," says Johnson. "I don't doubt you."

"They need structure and they need compassion."

"They need respect, too." Johnson says.

"They earn respect," Dawn says.

Johnson is rarely left speechless. Dawn is circling the halls, clipboard in hand and calling residents for Check-in.

Residents lumber in and lounge on the sofas in the dark living room. Everyone knows to avoid the soiled cushions and broken springs. Johnson sinks deep into the last seat available. In a moment of quiet he scans the faces in the room. Can it be that everyone looks like Johnny Cash? He blinks. He decides he didn't get enough sleep. Dawn wheels a chair out from the office. With her pen in the air she counts the number present. "We're missing one," she says.

"Phil," says Javier.

"Go ahead and do The Serenity Prayer without me." Johnson digs himself out. "I'll get Phil." He takes a brief detour out to the back porch for a couple of drags on an unfinished butt, then he taps on Phil's door. "Yo, man, it's group."

No response.

Johnson inches open the door and sees Phil, shirtless, sitting on his bed. He is large, but not muscular. He looks as if he might have been very strong once, probably did the weights thing in prison. Now, with big fleshy shoulders hunched and belly folded over the top of his jeans, he resembles a sagging buffalo. He raises his eyes without lifting his big head.

"It's check-in time, Phil. A chance to let us know how you feel."

"I don't feel like it," Phil says.

"That's a start."

"I'm not like the rest of these assholes," He scratches his chest. One hand finds a gray T-shirt in his wrinkled bedspread. "Judge ordered me here."

"Yea, I know. You're not the first."

"I'm just saying I don't buy this bullshit, somebody riding my ass every minute of the day."

Johnson nods sympathy. He sees that Phil is slowly complying and he wants to be careful not to tick the big man off. "There's a lot of bullshit," Johnson says, "but hell, look at your alternatives."

The shirt comes down over Phil's head. Slowly, stiffly he makes his way to the door, then with a ribald three-packs-of-filterless-a-day laugh he says, "I'd get drunk with you."

Phil falls into the seat Johnson had occupied. Johnson sits cross-legged on the floor. Aloud, Carl falters through a passage from the Big Book. Is it Step Two, or Three; the one about the Higher Power. Many in the room could recite the passage in their sleep, but all refrain because it is Carl's turn.

"I got a question," Phil says.

"Please wait," says Dawn. Carl drones on until Phil interrupts again.

"Who are you?"

"Wait," she says, she straightens in her chair, "Carl is not finished." Carl takes up the book again and struggles through another half-sentence.

"My question is," counter clock-wise, Phil meets every eye in the room, comes to rest on Johnson, "is this Higher Power higher than the cops?" Johnson grimaces, shakes his head.

Dawn says, "One more disruption from you and there will be consequences."

Javier perks up, "He's already on blackout. Whadya gonna do?"

"Double blackout," Paulie says cheerfully.

"I'm gonna kick some punk ass," Phil tries to rise out of his seat, but it's difficult and he's halted by Johnson's quiet pronouncement.

"You're out of line, Phil. Cool down." Johnson looks at Dawn and he's afraid what she might say and what consequences might follow. "Let's get onto the goals thing. I think we're running late anyway," he says. The screen door bangs, it must be Trish already. "Kick it off, Carl."

"I want to call my sponsor."

"Good," says Johnson. "Joy?"

"I want to call my sponsor, too."

"OK, Angela?" says Dawn. She smiles enormous.

"I'm starting a diet today. I'm going to look irresistible in my new one-piece." Angela does a little shimmy with her shoulders, a grin for Francis.

"Very good, wonderful." Dawn slides forward on her seat. "How about you, Francis?"

"I'm going to have to take a cold shower," he says. Everyone laughs. Johnson breathes relief. "No," Francis adds, "I guess I'm going to think about getting in shape, too. Summer's here."

"Ruby? What's your goal today, Ruby?"

"Same as yesterday. I just want to hold it together."

"Good," Dawn says, "Dorsey?"

"I got an appointment with SSI. And I'm going to get myself a sponsor."

"Wonderful. Lou?"

Lou is new and still frightened of speaking in the group. His lower jaw moves but no words come. "Do you want us to come back to you, Lou?" Johnson asks.

"You must have some goal?" Dawn says, a tone that makes Johnson's teeth hurt. Phil sits back in his hole, closes his eyes.

After a very long pause, "Express myself," Lou manages.

"Good," says Dawn. "Very good. Kit?"

"I'm going shopping, some boots I saw in the newspaper."

"Marvelous. Javier?"

"Well," Javier leers at Francis, then Paulie, "I'm looking forward to getting to know, you know, the new staff." There's some snickering, an awkward pause.

"O-kay," Dawn says, her voice rising. "Gordon?"

"I have a lot of laundry to do."

"And how about you Phil?" All eyes turn to Phil, whose eyes are closed.

Trish pokes her head through the doorway from the office into the living room. "Morning everyone," she says. She gives Dawn a warm smile. "Don't let me interrupt."

"Phil?" says Dawn.

"Nothing," Phil growls.

Johnson stands, slaps his legs, "Well," he says.

"You can do better than that," Dawn says.

Phil thrusts his big head and shoulders forward, puts his elbows on his knees. He makes his eyes wide and glares at Dawn. "I want to get a twelve pack of Miller Genuine Draft, an eightball, and I want to find my fucking brother who stole my fucking Harley—"

"All right," Trish says very loudly. She walks to the center of the room. "Phil you get blackout. Meeting is finished."

The three staff take seats in the office for pass-on. Trish pulls the door shut. "He's out of here," she huffs. "I've had it with him."

"He's not at all interested in recovery," Dawn says.

"You just met him," Johnson says. "How can you know?"

"No, Johnson, no. Dawn's right. And you're not helping."

Five, six, seven years ago Johnson had strong convictions about helping people. He read all he could find on social group theory and he had a broad vision, change on many levels. Words like advocacy and empowerment used to stir something. Recovery was a complex and provocative idea in a society that promotes illness in so many ways. Johnson used to dream of creating a real treatment community with real self-esteem building through real work based upon real goals. Maybe Braddock had sold out or maybe he was the one that dared to be real, but Johnson simply soured and Trish was right—he wasn't helping. Occasionally a resident here or there would serve to rekindle some of the old spirit. Ruby stirred feelings of tenderness, pity. Phil, this whole thing with Phil, has made Johnson angry.

"Look," Johnson says, "he's not out of here. That's only two blackouts, right?"

"He's out of here as soon as Ted says so," Trish says.

"Well, maybe I'll talk to Ted," Johnson says. "I will." But he has no intention of talking to Braddock. The two haven't exchanged more than hello in months. In their last conversation Ted had advanced an opinion about the new Robert Cray album and when Johnson disagreed, the manager countered with such a tone of authority. Not only was he the boss, but now the bastard thinks he knows more about blues. There was no way

Johnson would willingly request Braddock's support on a treatment issue.

"You can bet I'm going to talk to him, too," Trish says.

"Me, too," Dawn says.

Some residents grab snacks, one makes a rush for the phone, several return to their rooms to finish dressing, and the others assume their relaxation posts. In fifteen minutes there will be exercise. Joy, Francis, Angela, Paulie, and Javier surround the table on the porch, their smoke turning white in the dull white sky. Ruby paces on a thin brick walkway between the parking lot and a field of dandelion grass. Just beyond is a patio, next to it a vegetable garden which has yet to be turned. Phil sits and smokes on the patio. Johnson feels a rush of energy, a sudden breathlessness, warmth in his cheeks—it's an idea, a very big idea that keeps expanding. He returns to the office. He can hear Dawn speaking in a confidential voice, and if there could have been any doubt, the way she smiles when he enters makes it clear she was speaking about him. He doesn't care. "Excuse me," he says. "Trish, where're the keys for the shed?"

"I sure don't know. Why?"

"I'll tell you why."

"Tell me."

"Cause I want to turn the garden."

Trish picks up a heavy wad of metal from the desktop. She rolls it in her hand. "It's got to be one of these." She tosses.

Johnson shakes the keys, tambourine percussion. He's buzzing from his idea. "Listen," he says, "Let me run the House Relations Group. I'm going to get Phil to contribute."

"It's too late, Johnson. My mind's made up."

"Just wait and see." The two women look dully at Johnson. "He'll surprise you. I promise."

Trish shrugs, looks at Dawn. Johnson bounds through the kitchen out to the porch. He overhears Bruce speaking to Paulie, something about, "Let go, Let God," and something about, "recovery is hard work," and he thinks there might be a contradiction but he doesn't want to get sidetracked. "Morning, Bruce." His idea is growing, growing, beyond words. "How you doing there, Ruby?" He fears it will slip away from him like this morning's dream. Nervously, he tries key after key in the shed's lock. It's as much about treatment as it is about art. It's about respect and it's about love. A key turns and in the dark moist of the shed, smell of rust and potting soil, he finds a spade. "It's about Phil's recovery and my own," he whispers to himself.

Johnson chooses a corner of earth ten feet from where Phil sits hunched, puffing smoke, and he sinks his shovel head three-quarters into the gravelly dirt. "Miller Genuine Draft," he grunts, "for me it's always been an icy Bud." Phil looks up. "Especially after a hard day's work."

"Bud tastes like water," Phil says. He laughs, "Not like I'd turn one down right now."

"To each his own," says Johnson. He turns the shovel and chops. "My old lady," he says, he'd never referred to his fiancee this way, "used to keep a garden. I used to bust my ass out there in the sun, for her, you know, because she loved it."

"Got another one of them rollies?" Phil says. "I'm out of smokes." Johnson tosses his pouch.

"You can roll 'em, can't you?"

"Shit yea. You learn something in the joint."

"Yea, well," Johnson says, "at least you learned something."

"I learned plenty, believe me."

"Yea?"

Here comes Dawn, again with the clipboard. "Come on you guys, it's exercise time," she calls.

"You want to do knee bends?" Johnson whispers to Phil.

"Fuck no."

Johnson quickly grabs a metal rake from the shed. "Phil's going to help me," he says.

"I'm not sure," Dawn holds the clipboard in two hands at her waist. "I guess that'd be OK." She waddles back into the house.

"So what else did you learn in prison?"

"Give me that shovel," Phil says. He puts his cigarette on the edge of an aluminum pie plate ashtray. With a Harley starting kick he sinks the spade deep in the dirt. "You can't bend over the way you're doing it, unless you want to ruin your back." Johnson watches. "And if you think about it, you're better off hosing the ground before you start turning your dirt. Not too much though, cause you don't want clumps." Johnson nods.

"I'll get the hose." Johnson sprays while Phil digs. With every turn of the shovel, Phil proffers a piece of wisdom about proper care of the soil and efficient methods of weeding, but he surprises Johnson when he says, "So what happened with you and your, um, girlfriend?"

"I blew it," Johnson says. Now he surprises himself. "I was too fucking selfish."

Phil flashes a look of recognition, suspicion. He lets the shovel fall in the dirt. He returns to his seat and his smoke. "Selfish is the only way to be," he says. "Any other way is stupid."

Ted Braddock rolls into the lot, shiny blue Camry. This is not what Johnson wanted, not at all. The windshield glares. There is an authoritative crunch from the emergency break. Braddock shifts his white lunch bag from left hand to right so he can look at his watch. "Morning fellas," he's up onto the porch, "Time for exercise, isn't it Phil?" and into the house. Johnson suddenly feels very tired. He'll find a way to pass the remaining hours of work because he always does, but it will be dreadful.

"I've got to take a leak," he says. He leaves Phil puffing on the patio.

The regular staff gather in the office, talk of car payments and hot tubs and Dawn's got an endless story about her veterinarian, her laughter loud enough to match Braddock's. Johnson is outside paging through the sports section. He's trying to tune out the banter, mostly Paulie defending his manhood. "I don't care where he's been or how big he is, if he comes near me I'm gonna kick his ass." And Joy, peacemaker, "Maybe you'll get a room switch as soon as someone moves out." And savvy Javier, "Phil'll be the one to go. They ain't gonna put up with that."

Johnson imagines several things to say to Paulie, how the kid might re-examine his response, how it seems to fit a pattern. He might get the kid to think and speak realistically about what he'll do with his anger, and what his anger will do to him. This is a therapeutic opportunity, Johnson remembers, but what he feels most of all is sleepy. God grant me the wisdom…, he thinks, because nothing I say or do is going to make a damn bit of difference.

Dawn calls, "Group." She looks at the clipboard in her hand. "Step Study." She tells Johnson that Trish is going to let her run this one, that he can sit in if he likes. "No," he says, "I'd prefer not to." And thus goes the late morning and early afternoon: Johnson turns over some dirt until he's bored with it; he makes himself a bologna sandwich on white bread; he rolls and smokes seven cigarettes; he completes *The New York Times* and the *Press Democrat* crosswords; he plays horseshoes with Carl; he avoids Ted at all turns, except when he must go to the office to take charts out of the cabinet. Ted surprises Johnson with an enthusiastic, "How ya doing, Mike?" And Johnson mumbles back, "How ya doing?"

"Have you heard the latest John Lee Hooker? Takes me back." Braddock is working his plastic fork through a pile of chickpeas.

"No," says Johnson. "Not yet." He carries the heavy binders to the picnic table where he can leisurely scribble what he's observed.

It is nearly three o'clock when again Dawn calls "Group!" from the screen door. "Look lively!" The residents trudge in. Johnson holds the door and follows Phil, the last. "Look lively,"

Phil says. Trish is already in the living room. "Go ahead, it's your show," she says to Johnson.

"What?" he says. "Forget it," he says. "Let Dawn do it."

"It's yours. You asked for it," Trish says, "but wait just a minute because Ted wants to sit in."

It's a full house, minus Bruce who files paper and takes calls in the office. Johnson takes the tall chair on wheels, Trish beside him. Though it's meant to be a circle, he feels very much in the center. Phil sits deep in the sofa, a tight squeeze between Ruby and Joy. He puts his big buffalo head in his hands, eyes down.

"Welcome to House Relations," Johnson says. It is indisputably the most unpleasant of the groups, worse even than Addiction Awareness. It's a bickering session about dirty dishes left in sinks and refrigerators. Nothing ever improves as a result. "If it's OK with the higher powers," Johnson nods in the direction of Braddock seated on a folding chair by the office door, "I'd like to abandon the usual format. Rather than go around the circle and have everyone say what gets his goat, let's do it like a conversation. Someone starts and others join in when they have something to say."

"That's all right with me," Braddock shrugs, "so long as everyone says something."

"I like it this way better," Javier says.

"Good, now who's got what?" Johnson looks at the Zee of light cutting through the blinds across Paulie's neck and face. Paulie examines the cartoon faces he's drawn on the tips of his Converse high-tops. Braddock looks up at the clock on the wall behind Johnson.

"I don't like people touching me when I don't want to be touched," Ruby's hugging her thin arms around her knees in front of her chest.

"Neither do I," Angela says.

"Sometimes I like a hug," Joy looks thoughtful, "but I don't like people coming up from behind and putting their hands on me. It gives me the creeps."

"I don't do hugs," Phil says.

"Let's back up," Johnson faces Ruby. "Do you want to say who's touching you, or would you rather not say?"

"He knows who he is."

"Anyone else?" He looks at Angela, then Joy, but it's moot because most heads have turned to Javier.

"Javier, is there anything you want to say?" Johnson's voice is soft, unaccusing.

"I don't mean anything by it. Where I come from people touch people all the time. It's just being friendly." There is another moment of quiet while the room considers this.

"It doesn't seem that it's being taken as a sign of friendship," Johnson says.

"It's not that bad," Joy says, "so long as he doesn't come up from behind."

"You might sometimes accept an embrace from Javier? If you can see it coming, that is."

"Sure," Joy says. "Javier is my friend. But I also know what Ruby is talking about."

Ruby puts her feet on the floor and her hands in her lap. The sliver of light finds her cheeks glistening. "I get lonely, too," she says. She's present and she's long ago. She twists a rope of her hair around two fingers. "Maybe I know how you feel, Javier. I'm just not ready to be touched. I had too much of that, you know, when I didn't want it." Her wet eyes flash to Johnson, then to the carpet and rise slowly back up to Javier.

"I hear you," Javier says, and he does and everyone knows it because you can't not hear Ruby on the occasions when she opens up. What could possibly come next?

"Thank you," Johnson says. "Do we want to go deeper with this, or do we want to move on?"

"I said I don't do hugs," Phil says, still with head in hands.

"I see," Johnson says. What he sees is a trap. A work of sabotage. He sees Phil in one of a million angry moments vindicating Trish's distrust, Dawn's superiority and Braddock's self-serving perpetuation of the status quo. He feels like a fool, but he must proceed. "And has that been a problem for you here? Hugs?"

"No," Phil says.

"Well then, the floor is open."

"Cause I don't want nobody touching me," Phil says. "I don't want nobody in my business."

"I understand," says Johnson. "Maybe I was off base this morning. I saw you blowing this program and I guess I wanted to get a sense of what's important to you."

"That's right you were off base," Phil says. His eyes shoot to Braddock. "I used to hug," He lifts his head until he is facing Johnson, "I remember a time when I cared about things like gardens," very tentatively his gaze turns the circle until it settles on Paulie, "and staying sober, though it was always fucking hard. I used to think that everything mattered, especially keeping my bike tuned and keeping my friends. I used to have friends."

Now everyone is stunned. Paulie breaks the quiet. "What happened?"

"I don't talk about that," Phil says. "Not yet, kid."

"Someday, maybe," Johnson suggests.

"Yea, maybe."

"I get angry," Javier says, "when I feel like something's been taken away from me. Something that was mine."

"Like what?" Joy asks.

"Like what?" says Ruby.

"Like my family in Mexico," he says. "They can't come here. And if I go there I can't get the money to pay for the medicine I need."

"I don't think I've ever seen you angry, Javier. You must have some way of showing it," Johnson says.

The room considers. Trish taps Johnson's elbow and whispers in his ear, "I think we're getting away from House Relations."

"Let's see where it leads," Johnson whispers back.

And Phil says, "I get you," to Javier, "about something being taken away. There's always some bastards—"

Ruby cuts in, "Stolen."

And Johnson says, "Or forfeited." He doesn't mean to look at Ted Braddock when he asks, "Can you ever get it back?"

Kit and Angela try to speak at the same time and after embarrassed laughter they both persist.

"I lost it when my child was taken from me," Angela says. Her face melts with the words, "My little girl." Joy strokes Angela's forearm, takes her hand and squeezes it.

"You know," says Kit, "I had everything I wanted. It wasn't ever enough."

Once more Trish taps Johnson and he whispers, "It's my show." Braddock pulls his chair into the circle to listen closely, perhaps to speak, but he'll have to wait his turn because it is Johnson's show, Johnson back-up singer, Johnson song writer, Johnson blues man, he's never heard the notes so precisely, and on it goes, without a single reference to dirty dishes in sinks and refrigerators, his show, just one sweet, sad, honest riff laid down upon another. Johnson's long shift is almost finished and yet it seems he's only started.

ACKNOWLEDGMENTS

Grateful acknowledgment is made to the editors of the following magazines in which these stories first appeared:

Aphasia ("Mr. Passion")
Conduit ("Toxic Roundup")
Crack ("White Veil")
Fine Print ("The Smilies Meet the Brooders")
Fourteen Hills: SFSU Review ("What to Say When You Talk to Yourself")
other voices ("The Resolution of Nothing")
Our Working Lives Series from Bottom Dog Press ("Double Shift")
The Prairie Star ("Transactional Paralysis")
Savannah Literary Journal ("A Day at the Beach")
Six Thousand Five Hundred ("How We Remember You")
Thin Air ("Where's Fran Hayes?")
Zone 3 ("New Job")
ZYZZYVA ("The Right Hand Man")

Thank you Susan and Circe for wrestling matches, hide and seek, and uncountable sacrifices while these stories were being dreamed. Thanks Rick, Val, Meem, the people you love and the people who love you. Thanks to friends and teachers in the creative writing department at SFSU, especially Maxine Chernoff, Michele Carter, Molly Giles, Alissa Blackman, Ruth Goldstone, Alex Green. Thanks Rosellen Brown. Thanks Terry Furry. Thanks to all the kind helpful staff of Helicon Nine, especially Gloria Vando Hickok, Betsy Beasley, and Deb Kroman. Thanks Lawrence Coshnear, Jerry Nitzberg, Steve Elder, Nava Renek, David Porter for thoughtful readings and honest responses. Thanks again to David Porter for helping to clean the interior of my car and a thousand other things. Thanks Jim@exoteric.org for guiding me into this century. Thanks Stefan for babysitting, lunches with sprinkles. Thanks to the Guerneville Post Office.

A NOTE ON THE AUTHOR

Daniel Coshnear grew up in Baltimore, grew older in New York City, and now lives with his wife, Susan, and daughter, Circe, in Guerneville, California, beneath towering redwoods, and several stones' throws from the Russian River. He was awarded a Henfield Prize in 1997 for "How We Remember You." He received an MFA from San Francisco State University in 1998. He is a part-time instructor at SFSU Extension and also through the UC Berkeley Extension. He works night shift at a group home for men and women with mental illness and substance abuse. He is also fiction editor for a new litmag called *20 Pounds of Headlights. Jobs & Other Preoccupations* is his first book.

RECENT BOOKS BY HELICON NINE EDITIONS

FICTION

Toy Guns, a first collection of short stories by Lisa Norris.
1999 Willa Cather Fiction Prizewinner. Selected by Al Young.

One Girl, a novel in stories by Sheila Kohler.
1998 Willa Cather Fiction Prizewinner. Selected by William Gass.

Climbing the God Tree, a novel in stories by Jaimee Wriston Colbert.
1997 Willa Cather Fiction Prizewinner. Selected by Dawn Raffel.

Eternal City, a first collection of stories by Molly Shapiro.
1996 Willa Cather Fiction Prizewinner. Selected by Hilary Masters.

Knucklebones, a first collection of short stories by Annabel Thomas.
1994 Willa Cather Fiction Prizewinner. Selected by Daniel Stern.

Galaxy Girls:Wonder Women, a first collection of stories by Anne Whitney Pierce.
1993 Willa Cather Fiction Prizewinner. Selected by Carolyn Doty. Second printing.

Return to Sender, a first novel by Ann Slegman, is both tender and hilarious.

Italian Smoking Piece with Simultaneous Translation, by Christy Sheffield-Sanford.
A multi-dimensional tour de force.

POETRY

Lick of Sense, a first book of poems by Suzanne Rhodenbaugh.
2000 Marianne Moore Poetry Prizewinner. Selected by Alicia Ostriker.

The Air Lost in Breathing, a first book of poems by Simone Muench.
1999 Marianne Moore Poetry Prizewinner. Selected by Charlie Smith.

Flesh, a first book of poems by Susan Gubernat.
1998 Marianne Moore Poetry Prizewinner. Selected by Robert Phillips.

Diasporadic, a first book of poems by Patty Seyburn. Second printing.
1997 Marianne Moore Poetry Prizewinner. Selected by Molly Peacock.
2000 Notable Book Award winner for poetry (American Library Association).

On Days Like This, poems about baseball and life by the late Dan Quisenberry,
one of America's favorite pitchers.

Prayers to the Other Life, a first book of poems by Christopher Seid.
1996 Marianne Moore Poetry Prizewinner. Selected by David Ray.

A Strange Heart, a second book of poems by Jane O. Wayne. Second printing.
1995 Marianne Moore Poetry Prizewinner. Selected by James Tate. Received the
1996 Society of Midland Authors Poetry Competition Award.

Without Warning, a second book of poems by Elizabeth Goldring.
Co-published with BkMk Press, University of Missouri-Kansas City.

Night Drawings, a first book of poems by Marjorie Stelmach.
1994 Marianne Moore Poetry Prizewinner. Introduction by David Ignatow, judge.

Wool Highways, poems of New Zealand by David Ray. Received the
1993 William Carlos Williams Poetry Award (Poetry Society of America).

ANTHOLOGIES

Spud Songs: An Anthology of Potato Poems, edited by Gloria Vando & Robert Stewart.
Proceeds to benefit Hunger Relief.

The Helicon Nine Reader: A Celebration of Women in the Arts,
edited by Gloria Vando Hickok. The best of ten years of *Helicon Nine*.